OUT ON THE ICE

LANE HAYES

Cover Design by Reese Dante

Colby Fischer is a bad boy with attitude and a chip on his shoulder. As a senior in college, he knows this may be his last shot. He doubts he'll ever become the hockey legend he dreamed of being as a kid, but he definitely doesn't want to be an accountant. Things get interesting when he's asked to train the new intern at his step-dad's firm, who happens to be the one guy Colby can't stand.

Baseball is Sky Jameson's life. He's happy to be back at Chilton for his senior year, but he's burned a few bridges and has too much free time. He could use the money and something to keep him busy until his season begins. But his accidental crush on his prickly coworker could be a problem. Colby is straight and Sky is in the closet. Their timing isn't great, but the attraction is hard to deny. With his final season on the hockey team in the balance, Colby may have to decide if he's ready to come out on the ice.

For Brett- My original "justice leaguer"! I admire your courage, conviction, and integrity. May you always embrace your sense of truth and justice with an open heart and a curious mind.

1

"Ice burns, and it is hard to the warm-skinned to distinguish one sensation, fire, from the other, frost."—A.S. Byatt, *Elementals: Stories of Fire and Ice*

A SINGLE RAY of light streaked across the empty desk next to the window, hinting at blue skies, warm temps, and plenty of sunshine on the other side of the blinds. Pretty much the kind of weather everyone expected on an average summer day in SoCal. There was something undeniably torturous about being stuck in a classroom on a beautiful morning in July. Summertime wasn't supposed to be about school. It was reserved for fun stuff like body surfing, bike riding, and beach volleyball with your buddies. Or hanging out at the rink.

Anywhere but here.

Other than the perky brunette in the first row who talked my ear off about applying the principles of macroeconomics in virtual consumer bases on the first day of class, the other dozen or so students probably checked the time as often as I did. It wasn't a lack of interest. It was just...summertime.

Truthfully, I kinda liked econ, and I was a pretty good at it. It took extra qualifications to be accepted into this advanced course; a recommendation from two professors and an internship. I got the recs okay, and I interned at my stepdad's accounting firm. According to my mom, it was a brilliant move. I wasn't so sure about that—I wanted to play hockey and make bank, not worry about someone else's money.

The only person who seemed more miserable was the jock who arrived late every day and sat in the now-empty seat next to the window. I glanced from the door to my watch, knowing that any second now he'd barge in and—

"Welcome, Mr. Jameson. Nice of you to join us this morning," the TA commented sarcastically.

"Sorry, I'm late," he mumbled, rushing into the classroom.

"You're just in time for the quiz. Wait. Don't sit there. Maintenance is supposed to fix the leg on that desk. Take a seat next to Mr. Fischer."

"Who's Mr. Fischer?"

"Me." I raised my hand, giving Jameson a harsh once-over.

I didn't like the guy. Don't ask me why. He was just too... perfect. Super handsome and full of himself. I'd never seen him on campus before this summer. And maybe I had a slightly suspicious nature, but I couldn't help wondering what he was doing here. He looked a little out of place, more like a model than a student. No kidding. He could have been on a poster advertising the All-American athlete or an Abercrombie model with his dark-blond hair, blue eyes, broad shoulders, and a toned, muscular physique. Guys like him didn't take high-level summer school econ classes. They hung out at the beach with other beautiful people racking up content for their Instagram pages. Not Sky Jameson, though. He was here in hell with the rest of us, looking suspiciously unruffled in a snug black tee and khaki shorts. Every girl in the room and a few of the guys checked him out as he made his way across the room and settled into the desk next to me. Myself included. And yeah, that was weird.

I didn't think it was a gay or straight thing. It was—okay, fine. I didn't know what it was. For three weeks, I'd been staring at the back of the guy's head and noticing his biceps in those fitted T-shirts he wore and frankly, I was beginning to freak myself out. My fixation was odd. I thought about asking the pretty know-it-all in the front row for her number, hoping it would help me snap out of it. But when I stood up and brushed elbows with Sky, my mind went blank and I couldn't remember what the hell I was supposed to be doing. It would have been a dick move. I didn't want to mislead her or make her think I was interested. She already looked at me funny anyway.

Two and a half weeks of torture to go.

"It's test time!" The TA, whose name I never remembered... Mr. Jackson or Jackman or Jackoff, handed a stack of papers to a redheaded dude in the front row and gestured for him to take one and pass it around. "I'll give you thirty minutes to complete the quiz before we start a new chapter. We'll go over the answers tomorrow. You may use your calculators, but be sure to show all your work and of course, keep your eyes on your own paper and..."

I tuned Mr. J out as I pulled my calculator and a pencil from my backpack. These quizzes weren't usually difficult. A few multiple-choice questions followed by a detailed word problem or two involving statistics and some basic calculus. The trick was remembering to apply the correct formula. I scribbled a couple of notes, then flipped the paper over just as someone nudged my elbow.

"Hey, do you have an extra pencil?" Jameson whispered.

I stared at him in surprise for a second. I was pretty sure we hadn't spoken at all since summer school began. Close-quarter eye contact with someone as physically perfect as Sky was jarring. I wasn't a troll by any means; I just wasn't special. I was five eleven with shaggy brown hair, brown eyes, and a medium build. I never thought twice about what I wore or what anyone thought about my looks. Maybe Jameson didn't either, but that almost made it worse 'cause real people weren't supposed to look that good. It was…disconcerting. And why was he staring at me? What did he want? Oh, yeah.

I eyed him warily as I grabbed a pencil from my bag and handed it over. "Here."

"Thanks."

I grunted in response and got to work. I whipped through the multiple-choice questions, then read the word problems carefully, writing down the formulas I thought applied. The first one was easy, but the second one didn't compute. I mulled over possible formulas until I felt the weight of someone's stare. I cast a curious glance sideways just as Jameson averted his gaze.

"Are you cheating?" I hissed in a low tone.

He frowned, looking toward Mr. J before turning back to me with a sly, lopsided grin that doubled as a slick "What are you gonna do about it?" I furrowed my brow and craned my neck unthinking to see which of my formulas he copied.

"Mr. Fischer, please turn your quiz in."

I glanced up in confusion. "I'm not finished."

Mr. J crooked his finger meaningfully, then pointed at his podium at the front of the classroom. The rush of heat to my face was instantaneous. I felt like I'd opened an oven door and couldn't figure out how to close it fast enough. I was probably beet red and no doubt Mr. Jackoff would assume any flush of color was proof of my guilt.

Wrong. I was pissed.

I set the unfinished paper on the podium and did my best to

get my anger under control so I wouldn't say anything I might regret.

"You know the rules, Mr. Fischer. We have a zero-tolerance policy for cheating of any kind. Including wandering eyes," he said in a smug, grating voice that made him sound like someone's great-grandmother, which was funny 'cause I doubted he was thirty.

"My eyes weren't wandering. Check the jock sitting next to me," I replied loudly.

Mr. J narrowed his eyes sternly. "Take your seat, please."

I chewed the inside of my cheek angrily as I returned to my desk. I walked up the far aisle to avoid not-so-accidentally crumbling Jameson's test and shoving it down his throat. See? I had this anger thing under control.

I pulled my textbook out, practiced a few breathing exercises, and gave myself the same kind of pep talk I did before I hit the ice. *You got this. Stay focused. Keep it together. And above all... don't lose your shit.*

It worked. I got lost in numbers and variables and even memorized a new formula. By the time the test was over and regular instruction began, I'd compartmentalized my issue with the dickhead seated to my right. I ignored him and concentrated on the boring lecture like it was the play-by-play highlights from overtime of game seven in the league championships. And trust me, it wasn't.

The urge to gather my stuff and race to my car after class was strong. I told Elliot and the guys I'd meet them at the beach for a game of volleyball, but I figured I should maturely address the alleged cheating issue with the TA first. So I took my time, methodically stacking my notebooks and sliding them into my backpack as I watched Jameson with the cute brunette, aka Miss Smartypants, at her desk. He must have cracked a joke, 'cause she laughed hysterically, then followed him into the hallway. And he didn't spare me a second glance. *Fucker.*

Probably for the best. My temper was still on a high simmer, and I doubted that would change until I got off campus.

"Mr. Fischer. What can I do for you?" the TA asked with a friendly grin, as though he'd forgotten about the quiz fiasco.

I didn't bother trying to return the gesture. I had zero time or respect for phoniness in any form. Even a smile. I nodded curtly and got to the point.

"I'm not sure how you grade these quizzes, but I'm not taking this course to fail."

He regarded me thoughtfully and let out a parental-sounding sigh.

"Don't worry about the quiz. But I'd suggest you keep your eyes on your own paper in the future," he warned, grabbing his briefcase from under the podium and heading for the door.

I gritted my teeth and hiked my backpack over my right shoulder just as my cell buzzed in my bag. I paused to check the incoming text from our team captain. Something about a change in the preseason practice schedule. I typed a quick reply as I made my way to the exit. Then I slipped my phone into my pocket and immediately ran into a human wall.

"Hey. Here's your pencil. Thanks, man."

"My pencil?" I repeated. "Really?"

"Yeah. I was running late this morning, and you know how that goes." He gave a half laugh as he tapped the pencil against his palm. "I'm Sky, by the way."

I fixed him with a steady glare as I crossed my arms. "I don't give a fuck who you are. Why'd you do that?"

"Do what?" he asked, looking guilty as fuck.

"Cheat."

"I didn't cheat."

I widened my eyes comically and pointed at the scene of the

crime. "I was sitting right there. You were next to me and you never sit next to me, so yeah, I noticed. And when you—"

"Why would you notice that?" he interrupted.

The question caught me off guard. I cocked my head and studied him for a second. He tilted his head, and a lock of hair fell across his forehead. I fought a strange itchy compulsion to push it aside so I could see his eyes, 'cause damn, Sky was even better looking up close. He had a square jaw, high cheekbones, long eyelashes and—*oh, fuck.* That was weird.

I licked my lips and did my best not to stare at his tongue when he mimicked the motion. Like he was on to me. Like he knew something about me and was giving me a chance to figure it out on my own. Like he was somehow being cool, maybe even respectful. But that didn't make sense unless maybe he was...

"Are you coming on to me?"

Sky chuckled and pushed the eraser end of the pencil against my stomach. "No, I'm returning your pencil. Sorry you got nabbed for cheating, but c'mon...you were looking at me funny. Like you're doing right now."

"You mean like I can't believe how full of shit you are?" I snapped. "Don't try to turn this around. You know exactly what you did, asshole. Grow a pair and admit it."

He dropped the good-natured act so fast, I blinked. If I wasn't irritated and on my way to straight-up angry again, I might have been wary of the sudden change. Sky was taller than me and pretty buff, but I was thicker and more muscular, and I wasn't the type to back down from a fight. Ever. I held his gaze for a long moment. And just when I thought I was stuck in a staring contest, he lowered his eyes and fixated on my mouth before moving south. He lingered on my crotch and flashed a mischievous half smile.

"Okay. I admit it. I looked at you. But only because you looked at me first."

I huffed. "Nice try. You cheated and now you're lying and checkin' out my dick to distract me. Look, I'm not gay, and I don't care if you are, but—"

Sky held his hands up in mock surrender. "Relax. I'm wondering if you stuck a sock in your shorts or if you're just happy to see me."

I frowned. What was he up to? Was he *trying* to start a fight?

I let out a humorless chuckle. "I'm definitely not happy to see you, Jameson. I'm innocently waiting on my apology while you try to work out how big my cock is and if you can swallow it in—"

Sky launched himself at me. The impact knocked me sideways, pushing me into the first row of desks. When the back of my thigh scraped against metal, I saw red. I didn't think, I acted. I gripped his T-shirt with my left hand, cocked my fist, and swung. He pulled out of my hold before I connected with his jaw and used the momentum to his advantage, yanking my arm and throwing me off balance. I swayed like a tree in a storm, accidentally pulling him to the floor with me. Bad move. There was no space to maneuver between the rows of desks without wrecking the room.

I weighed my options as Sky flattened himself over me, grasping my wrists in a tight hold. His eyes blazed angrily, and his nostrils flared. My muscles tensed as I prepared to fend him off.

But he didn't do anything. He just stared at me. His gaze darted between my eyes and my mouth. Back and forth, like he was waiting for me to say something. He tightened his hold when I tried to wiggle free. I arched and tried again and...froze at the first slide of his hard shaft against mine.

Holy fuck.

I studied his expression for clues or a way out of this without embarrassing both of us, when my cock swelled against the

Velcro opening of my shorts. I didn't know what that said about me or him or anything. Before my mind went into overdrive, Sky jumped up and stood over me. And I was trapped.

I eyed his crotch for a second and closed my eyes briefly. I tried to refocus when my body betrayed me a little more. Why the fuck did I wear board shorts to class?

Sky snorted derisively and moved aside. He left me enough room to sit up, then extended his hand as though offering to help me to my feet. I swatted him away and glowered. He rolled his eyes, inching back when I scooted to my knees. The narrow aisle made it difficult to get to my feet gracefully. I reached for the nearest chair, but he held his hand out again. This time, I grabbed it...and he immediately let go.

"Oh, hey. Sorry about that."

"Fuck you." I pushed him hard as I stood, brushing myself off and casting a dirty look his way. "Stay the fuck away from me, asshole. Don't sit next to me, don't talk to me, and bring your own fuckin' pencil."

Sky studied me intently and smiled. One of those slow-growing lopsided grins I'd always associated with crazy people. "Whatever you say, Fischer."

He gave me a thorough once-over, lingering on my now obscene hard-on attempting to poke a hole through my board shorts. Then he picked up his backpack and moved to the door. I stared after him for a long moment, absently gripping my length through the nylon barrier. I'd been in enough fights on the ice and off to recognize the aftereffects of a sudden adrenaline rush. Erratic heartbeat, racing pulse, muscle tension...however, the boner was harder to explain.

I dropped my hand quickly, picked up my bag, and headed for the parking lot. I tossed my stuff into the back seat of my Prius and texted Elliot.

I'm bailin'. I need to get on the ice. Talk to you later.

I started the engine, glanced in my rearview mirror, and was about to back up when my cell buzzed. I put my phone on Bluetooth and answered, "Hey. Sorry. I can't make it."

"You're an asshole," Elliot huffed irritably. "What happened to 'I'll be there after class, man'?"

"Call Tucker. He's always up for a last-minute game," I suggested, pulling out of my parking spot. "I gotta run. See ya—"

"Hold up! What's wrong?"

"Nothin'. Why?"

"I know you too well, Colby. Who pissed in your cornflakes? Harry?"

"Harry? No. Just...some dick at school."

Elliot snort laughed. "A hairy dick?"

I sighed theatrically. "You're hilarious, El."

I filled him in on my run-in with Sky, leaving out the fact that I was, in fact, still half-hard from the encounter. Not that Elliot would be fazed. My best friend-slash-roommate was famous for coining phrases like "contact chubby" and "insta-chub" in junior high school. Definition...an immediate and embarrassing erection that results from unintentionally rubbing your junk against an opponent. We'd died laughing but both agreed it was a real phenomenon. Elliot was a volleyball player, so even though I kinda doubted he ever got much "accidental contact," he got away with saying weird shit 'cause he was clever as fuck and funny too. He was also a fiercely protective friend. Elliot stuck with me through some of the crappiest times in my life. I trusted him implicitly and when he recently came out as bi, I made sure he knew I had his back.

But I didn't want to talk about Sky and give Elliot the idea that our encounter was anything besides annoying.

"Let it go, Colb. You've got a couple of weeks of geek school left, and you can literally skate through senior year. Nothing to worry about except showing off for the scouts and deciding which NHL offer to accept," Elliot said.

"Oh sure, 'cause that's exactly how it'll go." I huffed sarcastically as I turned left onto 7th Street. "I'm hanging up now. Go find a fourth. See you after practice."

"Not tonight. I got a date."

"A date? Like with a person or are you talking about those raisin things that look like dried up cockroaches?"

Elliot snickered at my lame attempt at humor. "A person date."

"Hmm. Who is she?"

"Not she...*he*. His name is Drew."

"Drew," I repeated.

I slowed behind a red Jeep and studied the bumper stickers covering the rear window while I tried to think of a polite and proper reply. My hesitation had nothing to do with a lack of support. This was just the first time Elliot talked about going out with a guy. It was new.

He'd been with Anna for three years until he broke up with her last May. They'd been one of those weirdly mature couples. The type who meal-planned, went grocery shopping every Sunday, and recorded their favorite shows on each other's TVs even though they didn't live together. Most twenty-two-year-old college students didn't do that shit unless they were committed in a "We're going to get married eventually anyway" sense. But hey, don't listen to me. The only thing I'd ever seriously been committed to was hockey. Period.

"Yeah. We met at that seafood place by the pier. He's a waiter and he's funny and yeah...I asked him out and he said yes," Elliot said conversationally.

"Right. Okay. Um...well, have fun."

"Thanks. Talk to you later."

I stared at the traffic light in a daze when he ended the

connection. I wasn't sure what to make of my world at the moment. Everything felt upside down. I set my sunglasses on my nose when the light turned green and cranked up the volume on a Beck classic. Somewhere in between the harsh notes of a screaming guitar, I remembered my dad's advice. When in doubt, skate.

When I was a kid, I'd wanted to be an Olympic speed skater. No joke. Our neighbors back in Michigan owned the local rink. I had a standing invite to goof around on the ice…as long as there was an adult to supervise. Since my dad worked odd hours at the plant, he was usually the one to keep an eye on me while the Gorskis got the rink ready for after-school lessons and team practices.

I had vivid memories of being five years old and rushing to tie my skates as fast as possible to get out there before anyone marred the pristine ice. I could still hear my dad telling me not to forget my gloves as I ran on my blades, purposefully building momentum, then gliding across the glassy surface. Once I got going, I didn't want to stop. I would skate circles around the beginning figure skaters, zipping forward and backward as I lost myself in the sheer joy of unfettered speed. I was fast, agile, and sure-footed. Thankfully, those were good qualities for a hockey player too.

I'd always liked hockey, but it became an obsession after a kid in my third grade class invited me to a Red Wings game. I loved the energy and the intense atmosphere. It was fast-paced and a little wicked. Okay, a lot wicked. I lost track of the number of fights we witnessed that night. The last one was the best—every member of both teams was on the ice, duking it out while the crowd went nuts. I wanted a piece of the action. I wanted to see my name flashing on the Jumbotron in a crowded arena. I wanted to be the next Sidney Crosby. No...the next Wayne Gretzky.

A few years later, my life went to hell. Dramatic, I know, but true. My parents divorced when I was thirteen. My mom moved to Long Beach, leaving Dad and hockey behind. Sure, they had hockey in Southern California, but joining a club team cost money my mom didn't have until she met Harry. I lost two years on the ice to sports like volleyball and basketball that required nothing more than a ball and a friend. I met Elliot, so I couldn't really complain. But then my mom married a rich old man, my dad died, and my world as I knew it ended. I lost everything. The only silver lining was that I got hockey back. And though I resented Harry and hated that he was in my life and my father wasn't, I thought my dad might have been looking out for me somehow. It was up to me to make something of it.

Seven years later, my pro hockey dream wasn't on track. Sure, I was fast, accurate, and I'd been told I had leadership skills. But I wasn't special. And at this point, I'd be cool with knowing what the hell I was going to do when I graduated, I mused as I raced to catch up to Logan's lame-ass drop pass.

"Oops."

"What the hell?" I griped, driving the puck forward a few feet on the edge of my stick before passing it to my teammate.

Logan steamed toward the goal with purpose. Troy crouched low in the cage but kept his gaze on me as though anticipating another pass in my direction. He shifted to his right when Logan slid the puck to me. I closed the distance, drew back my stick at the last second, and shoveled it to Logan for the score.

"Woohoo!" Logan pumped his stick in the air in triumph. "Troy, my man, you fall for that one every fuckin' time."

I chuckled when Troy whipped his glove off to make a rude gesture, then tilted my head meaningfully at the group of kids entering the rink. "Watch your fuckin' mouth, Troy. And maybe consider taking a coupla passing lessons with the Pee Wee League. You're not flippin' burgers out there. Do it like you mean it."

"Hey, my bad. I don't know my own strength sometimes. That's why we're here...hours before practice." Logan waited a beat and added, "In July. Or did you get wind of Schultz and the scout?"

Troy and I turned to the stands and spotted our forward chatting with Coach Beltram and an older man behind the tall plexiglass barrier.

"When did that happen?" I asked.

"I don't know, but it must be recent. Schultz must have a big-time agent. That's how Stanley got picked up by the Ducks last year," Logan said.

"Yeah, and Stanley isn't half as good as either of you. Well... he's not as good as Fischer, anyway."

"Fuck you," Logan snorted without heat. "Let's grab a beer. I told Kelly I'd swing by her place after."

"After what...you jack off to some porn?" Troy taunted as he swept the puck from the cage.

Logan smacked Troy upside the helmet and skated out of reach.

I hung back and watched them, unseeing for a moment, then glanced over at the stands again just as Schultz and the mystery man walked off, leaving Coach behind. I sensed his stare, but I didn't acknowledge him. We were far enough away to size each other up without having to fake polite chitchat.

Good thing too, 'cause I wasn't sure what I'd say to him. "What the fuck?" worked, but my pride stopped me from making a fool of myself. Besides, my maturity had already been tested once today, and I was still reeling from it. I'd hoped an impromptu workout at the rink with some buddies would chase away old demons and keep me focused. But damn, I felt overwhelmed. And invisible.

And okay…a little jealous too. Which might have pissed me off the most 'cause Jason Schultz was a fine player. If a scout was interested in him, that was awesome. Really fucking awesome.

I took a deep breath and skated toward the exit, pausing to help one of the juniors up when he tripped over his blades and fell on his face while going after the puck. Poor kid was probably somewhere around nine. He looked miserable, like he wanted to cry. I could relate.

I dusted my gloves off and held my hand up for a high five. Then I skated toward the exit, flopped onto the metal bench outside the door, and bent to untie my laces. The temperature shift from the rink to the sweaty locker room was jarring in the summertime. I yanked my jersey over my head, pushed the locker room door open, and groaned.

"…moving fast, but I'm excited," Schultz enthused.

"Congrats. That's awesome, man. Put in a good word for the rest of us," Logan replied.

"Well, he watched you out there just now," Schultz said.

"That was a shootaround for fun. It didn't count," Troy huffed indignantly.

"Yeah, yeah. Coach mentioned it. He told him you guys were decent and that Fischer was a natural-born teacher."

"What's that supposed to mean?" I asked in greeting as I pulled my skates off and tossed them onto the ground beside my locker. "Congrats, by the way."

Schultz grinned. "Thanks. You know, Coach thinks you could take his place someday. You're all about mechanics, Fish. Why are you looking at me like that? It's a good thing."

I rolled my eyes, casting a cautious glance around the empty locker room before studying my teammates. Of the three of them, I had the most in common with Logan. We were both entering our fifth year of college, and I knew he sensed the same sort of pressure I did to figure out what came next. But Logan was an optimist. He took life in stride and was fond of saying things like, "Everything will work out." It probably would for him. Logan was six two with light-brown hair and green eyes. We called him a chick magnet 'cause girls gravitated to him everywhere he went. Not that he noticed. He was clueless when it came to that kind of stuff.

Troy was a junior. He was super intense and crazy competitive about odd things. For example, he'd celebrated his twenty-first birthday a month ago and was on a quest to exercise his newfound right to order alcohol at every bar in town...even though he never finished a whole beer. Troy was my height with brown hair and brown eyes. He was one of those unremarkable-looking people who became interesting the second he started talking—you never knew what the hell he'd say next.

But Schultz was the real deal. He left every piece of himself on the ice every time he played. I'd be happier for the guy if I liked him a little more. However, it was hard to like a guy who made cracks about the "proficiency of my mechanics." Who said shit like that? I didn't trust him as far as I could throw him. Which was nowhere. He was a six-foot-three brick house of a dude with Nordic good looks: blond hair, blue eyes, and a square jaw. He kind of reminded me of Sky, although Sky was godlike, handsome, and—okay...not good.

I flashed a tight-lipped smile at Schulz and huffed. "Every time you give me a compliment, I end up looking for the license plate of the truck that hit me."

"You're a paranoid psycho, Fischer. Being good at anything is a positive." Schultz bumped fists with Troy and Logan, then came to stand in front of me. He punched my bicep lightly, lowering his voice for my ears only when he continued. "But being great is better."

I clenched my jaw as I turned to deal with my lock, biting back the strong desire to check his ass into the wall of metal lockers. See what I mean? *Fucker.* I heard the lighthearted chatter as a few patrons entered, but I gave my full attention to changing my shirt before I grabbed my cell, closed my locker, and said a quick good-bye to my friends.

I scrolled through messages with my head down, pushed the glass door open, and stepped outside. I tossed my bag and my stick into the trunk just as my phone buzzed with an incoming text I hoped might lift my rotten mood. No such luck.

Hi Colby. I have good news! We signed a big client this afternoon. I'm going to need as much help at the office as possible. If you have any friends as smart as you in the econ department in need of part-time employment, send them my way. I'm happy to offer a referral fee as incentive. Hope you're having a terrific day. Talk to you later! All the best, Harry

I read the novel-length text message twice and slammed the trunk, sighing in defeat. What a crap day. Between cheating classmates, obnoxious teammates, and overly zealous step-dads…I was done.

I wished I'd blown off school and gone to the beach. If I'd skipped class, I wouldn't have gotten into that fight with Sky, and my day would have stayed on track. Maybe my bad mood wasn't entirely his fault, but he'd started a craptastic domino effect that made me think it would be in my best interests to stay far, far away from Sky Jameson.

OVER THE NEXT couple of weeks, I avoided Sky like the plague. I didn't look at him when he walked into the classroom or sneak peeks of him across the aisle. I kept my eyes on the professor or on my paper, turned in my work in a timely manner, and got the fuck out of there…fast.

Unfortunately, whatever he'd started the day he borrowed that stupid pencil hadn't gone away. I might not glance in his direction, but I felt his presence like a heavy blanket. My skin tingled and my heart accelerated like I was suddenly nervous or anxiety-ridden. Or…like I had a crush. And that was the part I didn't get. I couldn't have a crush. Not on a guy. I mean, maybe it was possible. But it had never happened before. And in T-minus ten minutes, I was pretty sure it would never happen again.

I completed my final exam with time to spare, double-checked my answers, and handed the test in. I spotted Sky in my periphery as I opened the door. If I hurried, I could escape without running into him. I rushed down the hallway, rounded the corner, and…*bam!* I ran into a professor carrying a stack of textbooks.

"Shoot. I'm sorry," I said, bending to gather the books.

"Oh, that's all right. I know how it is. Last day of summer school is a big deal. You know, back in my day…"

Oh boy. We had a talker. Professor Barrett taught advanced levels of economics. He had a shock of messy white hair and always wore short-sleeved oxford shirts that looked to be two sizes too big. I didn't know for sure, but I thought he was in his midseventies. He was one of my favorite professors, known for his sense of humor and rambling stories. Which made him literally the worst person I could have run into 'cause any second now Sky was going to—

"Hey, Colby. Got a minute?"

Fuck.

I pasted a smile on my face, handed Professor Barrett the books, and turned to Sky. I aimed for passively friendly, but it was a total fail. My heart did that skip-and-flip thing, and my mouth went dry. I didn't get it at all, and I didn't want to analyze it. I just wanted to get away from him.

"Um, I'm kinda busy right now..."

Professor Barrett patted my shoulder and grinned. "I'm quite all right. Talk to your friend, Mr. Fischer. You boys have a nice day and enjoy your last two weeks of summer."

Sky thanked the older man, then leaned against the wall and smirked. Or maybe it was a smile; I couldn't tell with him. "Gee, I wonder why he thinks we're friends."

"Trust me, I didn't spread any rumors. What's up?" I asked, noting that his snug blue T-shirt made his eyes pop. I was pretty sure I'd never thought twice about that sort of thing in my life. But just before I freaked myself out, he did it for me.

"I heard you're training me Monday afternoon, and I thought we should call a truce and maybe start over again." Sky's smiled widened as he offered his hand.

"Huh?"

Sky lowered his hand and squinted. "You're training me for the job."

"What job? What are you talking about?"

"Assistant analytic advisor...Bailey, Barnes, and Cohen. Ring any bells? I applied for the position and spoke to Harry Cohen's secretary. He called me back himself, offered me the gig, and asked if I knew his son. I didn't know he was your dad, but—"

"Harry's not my dad," I intercepted.

"Okay. Well, he said you might be in one of my classes. I couldn't figure out who he meant until he described you. Then I was like, 'Oh yeah. That's the guy who accused me of cheating.' " He paused to scowl at me. "I didn't cheat, by the way. I never cheat. I tried to talk to you a couple of times, but you've ignored me pretty hard."

"I didn't ignore you," I lied.

"Yeah, you did," he scoffed. "But if we're going be working

together, it's probably a good idea to clear the air. What d'ya say?"

Nothing. I had nothing to say. I was speechless. This was like winning the reverse lottery. What were the chances that out of the hundreds of students in the econ department, Harry would hire the one guy I didn't want anything to do with? *Fucking Harry.*

I narrowed my gaze. "Why?"

"Why...what?"

"Why everything?" I threw my hands in the air and paced a couple of steps away before I exploded. "Why that job? Why now? Who are you? Do you even go to school here? And call me crazy, but I think it's reasonable to be concerned about training the guy who cheated off my test to take over my position. Harry obviously doesn't know about that or he'd—"

"Sure, he does. I told him," Sky replied matter-of-factly.

"Whoa! You told Harry you cheated on me, and he still hired you?"

"Yeah, but we're not boyfriends, and I didn't go home with another guy," he teased, quirking his lips in amusement.

My mouth dropped open. *Boyfriends?* "What'd you tell Harry?"

Sky gave me a Cheshire cat grin and shrugged. "Nothing much. I said we had a misunderstanding."

"It was more than a misunderstanding," I snapped.

"Oh, come on," he scoffed. "It was bad timing, and you know it. I looked at you, you looked at me, and TA Dorkman looked at both of us at the same time...during a test. I'm sorry he called you out. I apologized to you afterward, but you were a little feisty. So I talked to the TA separately. He told me...and I quote, 'Mr. Fischer has not been penalized.' " Sky let out an amused half chuckle. "Just so you know, he enunciated every syllable so 'penalized' sounded like 'penis-sized.' I had to bite my tongue not to laugh and ruin the moment 'cause I was seconds away from asking if you either had a penis problem or needed dick."

His eyes sparked with ready humor. I studied his full lips and licked my own before meeting his gaze and...there it was again. That woozy, "butterflies in my stomach" feeling I'd only ever gotten around insanely pretty girls I didn't know how to talk to. Yeah, I knew what it meant. My body had gone rogue and decided it was okay to react to Sky the way I had around Sarah Bernardo our senior year of high school. She sat next to me in Trig and didn't give me the time of day until she needed help with an equation. I didn't take it personally. She was a popular cheerleader who hung out with the football crowd, and I played a sport she didn't understand. But I didn't trust people like her. Or Sky. Or anyone who used their looks to get what they wanted. And if I couldn't trust Sky, neither could Harry.

I smiled weakly and tried to think of a response to his penis quip, ideally without blushing or popping wood. It wasn't gonna be easy because I'd actually *felt* his dick...against mine, no less. And I hadn't hated it. That was the part that scared me most. Was I gay or bi or curious? Or just a guy on the verge of a nervous breakdown? And what were we even talking about?

Oh, yeah. The job.

"Why do you want to work for Harry?" I glowered.

"It's not personal. I need a job. My season doesn't start till January. I'm a fifth-year senior. I have two classes and way too much time on my hands. Oh yeah, and I'm broke. My student loans don't kick in until late August."

"Hmm. Still seems weird."

Sky huffed. "How is it weird? It's just a job."

"It's weird because I never saw you on campus before this summer. I don't know you, and I don't trust you. And Harry is too nice for his own good. He probably offered you something the second you said you were in my class. I bet he didn't ask any important questions."

"Sure, he did. We talked about software programs and analytic data and he asked about some econ theorems and…you know, accounting stuff," he said with an irritated shrug.

"Yeah, okay. But he obviously didn't cover the basics."

"Like what?"

I shot an annoyed look at him. "Like do you go to school here? Did you transfer? If so, why? What's your major? Where do you live? You look like an athlete. If so, what sport do you play? You know…questions to keep it real."

Sky furrowed his brow. "Is this a second interview or a date?"

"Very funny. If you want the job, start talking."

"I already got the job, asshole. Your dad hired me."

A red haze clouded my vision for a second. I curbed the intense desire to punch him and pushed him against the stucco wall instead. Hard.

"I told you he's not my fuckin' dad," I snarled, splaying my hand over his chest.

Sky didn't move a muscle. He stared at me intently, like he was trying to figure me out. Then he smiled. One of those condescending quirks of the lips that doubled as a sneer. The little fucker wanted to start something. It was like the classroom scenario all over again…only worse 'cause we were in public now. I couldn't lose my cool.

I let go of him and stepped away. I wasn't going to apologize or explain anything, but I had to say something. He beat me to it.

"Hmm. Noted."

"Just start talking. Who are you?" I demanded.

Sky cocked his head curiously and smiled. "If we're doing the 'date' thing and you want to get personal, you should ask me out. What are you doing right now?"

"Other than trying not to kick your ass...nothing. Why?" I asked suspiciously.

"I'm hungry. Let's grab a burrito at that Mexican place on Second Street," he suggested.

"Now?"

"Yeah. Now."

This time when he smiled, the butterflies turned into a flock of birds batting against my rib cage. I didn't get it. At all. This couldn't be a crush. That wasn't a real option 'cause I was straight and I didn't even like this guy. He was a jerk. A really good-looking one, for sure. But still a jerk. I studied his full lips, chiseled jaw, and high cheekbones for a moment, then looked away.

"Okay, fine," I heard myself say.

"Cool. Do you want to drive together? My car is in the front lot next to—"

"No. I'll meet you there. I don't want to be stuck with you. I can't stay long, and there's a good chance I'm gonna want to ditch your ass before your bean-and-cheese supreme arrives." I slipped my sunglasses over my eyes and hiked my backpack on my shoulder.

"Nah. You like me, Colby. You just don't know it yet." Sky fixed me with a mischievous lopsided grin as he stepped away from the wall. "See ya there."

2

Don't ask me why I agreed. I guess I was surprised by the invitation and then curious. And if Harry had really hired Sky to take my position while I was in season, it was practically my duty to find out more about him. Maybe an actual conversation with him would put an end to this strange feeling I got around him whenever he walked into a room.

I parked in the last available spot near a tall brick wall and walked along the pathway to the side entrance of the small Mexican eatery. La Mesa was more of a fast food joint than a real restaurant. You placed your order at the counter, took a number, and pounced on the first table available. Midweek at lunchtime could be tricky. I took my place in line and studied the menu above the register, grateful for the diversion. I didn't want to get caught staring at the front door like I was waiting for someone special. 'Cause that definitely wasn't the case. Sky might not show up at all. He seemed like the kind of asshole who'd suggest meeting for lunch and conveniently forget the time or the place.

"Hey." Sky bumped my elbow and inclined his head meaningfully. "Tell me what you want and grab a table. I saw one outside under an umbrella."

"You get it. I'll order."

"Okay. I'll have the number five with a side of guacamole and no *picante*. Make sure the avocados are fresh, though. Oh, and change the beans and rice to salad...dressing on the side." He shoved a twenty at me and started to walk away.

I grabbed his elbow before he could go anywhere. "What the fuck? I'm never gonna remember all that, and who the hell orders a salad with a burrito? You gotta get the rice and beans. It's a rule."

Sky snickered. "Says who?"

"Me and lots of other sane people."

"Fine. I'll do it myself. What do you want to eat?"

I shook my head as I stepped forward in line. "No, you get the table. I'll remember. Do you want a drink too?"

"A Diet Coke, but I don't trust you to order now."

"You can trust me."

"Okay, repeat my order."

"Not in public," I snarked.

Sky threw his head back and laughed. Fuck, that was a nice sound. Light and cheerful and easy. Which was funny because he didn't really seem like any of those adjectives.

"Don't mess it up, Fischer."

I furrowed my brow and pointed toward the door. Sky grinned, raised his hands in surrender, and walked away. I turned to study the menu unseeing before sneaking a peek at him through the window. The sun cast a golden glow over his hair and skin, giving him a godlike aura. I stared at his broad shoulders and his slim waist for a long moment, then licked my lips and moved forward in line. *Get a fucking grip. Sky is just a dude, and this is just lunch. No big deal.*

By the time I met him outside with our drinks and the

number for our order, I'd successfully talked myself off the ledge. I set his change next to his Diet Coke and slid into the metal chair across from him.

"That was embarrassing. Remind me never to order for you again," I huffed.

"Oh, I didn't realize we were making this a regular thing." Sky waggled his brows, snapped the top off his drink, and took a sip.

"We aren't. I'm not sure what we're doing."

"You're interviewing me, remember?"

"Right. By the way, the guacamole was from yesterday. It's a little brown, but if you swipe off the top layer, you'll never notice," I said as I tore the wrapper from my straw and popped it in my drink. "And they don't do salads, so I ordered you mashed potatoes...with gravy. You're welcome."

Sky snort laughed. "Thankfully, I know that's not true, but it's good to know the hockey player has a sense of humor."

"How'd you know I play hockey?"

"Lucky guess." He chuckled when I stared at him suspiciously. "Okay, fine. I saw you pulling ice skates and a hockey stick out of your trunk in the parking lot."

"Oh."

"You look like a hockey player."

"I'll take that as a compliment," I said.

Sky smiled then angled his head toward the restaurant. "Did you remember to hold the *picante*?"

"I remember everything," I replied unthinking.

He pursed his lips thoughtfully and somehow I knew he was thinking of that day in the classroom...the fight, the fall, him over me, and his cock nudging mine. I sucked on my straw and fixated on the posse of teenagers staring at their phones at the table next to ours.

"Is that an actual condition, or are you trying to impress me with weird bragging rights?" Sky shifted in his chair and bumped my leg.

I ignored the zing of awareness as I lowered my sunglasses. "I don't care about impressing you. I don't know you. And you're the one who's supposed to be impressing me."

"Are you always this big of an asshole?" he asked in a syrupy tone.

"Depends on who you ask. My mom thinks I'm sweet," I said. "What's the deal with you anyway? Tell me about yourself, and don't fuckin' lie. If you say one thing that isn't true, I'll report to Harry and make sure he doesn't hire you."

Sky held my gaze for a moment. "Dial back the dick routine. I didn't stage a takeover. I applied for a job. And I got it."

"Doesn't mean you get to keep it."

I leaned aside when a server delivered our lunch, then made a production of unwrapping my burrito while Sky asked about the red stickers covering the foil on his.

"I'm new here, but I guess it means extra spicy," the young man said with a bored shrug before moving on to the next table.

Sky glowered at me. "You sabotaged my order."

"My bad. I thought you liked it hot," I replied around a mouthful of food.

"I don't. Let's trade."

"Sorry, I can't do that. Spicy food makes me gassy. If I took one bite of that, you'd be super grateful we didn't drive together," I singsonged, impressed I was able to keep a straight face.

Sky rolled his eyes as he gingerly picked up his burrito. "Nothing gives away your age quite like a fart joke. How old are you?"

"Twenty-two. I'm a senior. You must be too, or you wouldn't be in that econ class."

"Unless I was a prodigy," he singsonged.

"Are you?"

"Nope. I'm a fifth-year senior at Chilton. I'm twenty-three."

I furrowed my brow. "The fancy private school in Orange? What are you doing at Long Beach State, then?"

"Playing catch-up. I dropped out at the beginning of winter semester last year, and I was too far behind to make up the work. My counselor suggested summer school, so here I am."

"Why here? Don't they offer econ classes during the summer at Chilton?"

"Yeah, but I can't afford them. I told you...my student loans don't kick in till late August. Thus the job," Sky said before taking a big bite of his burrito. "Mmm. This isn't bad."

I fixated on the corner of his mouth, fascinated by his ability to make chewing a fucking tortilla seem sexy. "It's what you ordered. I just told them to put 'Spicy' stickers on it."

He tilted his head curiously and smiled. "You're weird."

"I know. Keep talking. Do you live in Long Beach?"

"No."

"So, you plan on commuting every day from Orange?"

"Yep."

I gave him a sharp look. "Cut the one-word replies. I don't have time for twenty questions, and you aren't a guest on *Good Morning America*. Get talkin', Jameson. We don't have all damn day."

He looked like he was poised to unleash some serious snark, but he froze when he met my gaze...and something happened.

I suddenly felt breathless and lightheaded. I would have blamed it on the heat or exhaustion or any other lame excuse, except my dick swelled too. It was like there was an invisible conduit between his lips and my cock. The pull was so strong, I felt dizzy for a second.

"What's the matter?" he asked softly.

"Huh? What do you mean?"

"You look confused and a little spaced-out, like you just—"

"I'm fine," I intercepted. "Get talking. The job, the commute, Harry..."

"There's not much more to say. Except I start on Monday."

"This is your interview, part two. Take it seriously. Tell me your name, your birthday, where you were born, etcetera."

"What part of 'I already got the job' don't you get?" Sky huffed.

"What part of 'I'm gonna kick your ass if you don't cooperate' don't you get?"

He furrowed his brow angrily. "I can't tell if you hate me or if you hate that you like me. Whatever. My birthday is June twenty-sixth. I'm from Boise, but I'm newly emancipated from my family, so this is home now. I live in Orange and room with one of the guys on my team. Micah's a total pig. I'm gonna try to find another living situation ASAP, but it may have to wait till January. Hmm. Let's see...my dream job is to play shortstop for the Dodgers and my backup is something in finance. Don't ask me what. I don't want to think about it until March."

"What happens in March?"

"It's the halfway mark in my final season. If any scouts are interested in me, I'll know by then. If not, I need a real job." Sky sipped his Diet Coke. "What else do you want to know?"

I bit into my burrito and took my time chewing before asking, "What do you mean by emancipated?"

Sky made a slash across the throat motion. "*Adios, amigo.* Later, alligator."

I frowned. "Did your parents kick you out?"

"You could say that," he replied nonchalantly as he pulled his cell from his pocket and scrolled through his messages.

The not-so-subtle brush-off clearly indicated it was time to switch topics. That was cool. We weren't buddies. I only needed enough personal info to make sure he wasn't a psycho. Sky seemed harmless enough. In fact, he looked like a spoiled country club dweeb. The kind who wore striped V-neck sweaters and white jeans while they sipped champagne and chatted up girls with fake nails and plastic smiles. He had an air of entitlement about him that made me want to kick him in the nuts…or maybe just order extra hot sauce for his burrito. Yet he was sharp around the edges too. Something told me that big ol' chip on his shoulders was courtesy of some family bullshit. I could totally relate.

So I wasn't sure why I didn't let it go. "Why?"

He flashed a feral grin. "Is that really any of your business?"

"No. I'm just curious. Emancipation sounds so…legal. Like you divorced your parents."

"I guess I did." Sky regarded me thoughtfully, then glanced down at his cell. "So what else did you want to know? Let's see… I'm a *Star Wars* and *Star Trek* geek. I love comics too. Old ones. Batman is my favorite, which is weird 'cause I'm really more of a Marvel guy."

"Of course you are," I huffed derisively. "The movies are good, but DC has better superheroes…by far."

"Who? Superman?" he asked sarcastically.

"Yeah, and The Flash, Aquaman, Green Lantern…"

"You did not just say Green Lantern. That's embarrassing," he scoffed.

"Hey, Green Lantern is powerful."

"Yeah, but only if he's wearing a fuckin' ring. C'mon, that's hokey. Admit it."

I rolled my eyes. "Fine. But Batman makes up for all the lame ones. Not that it matters. We weren't talking about superheroes anyway."

"What were we talking about?"

"Your parents."

He lowered his gaze and tapped a message on his phone

dismissively. "I'm done talking about parents. Unless you want to talk about yours."

"No, thanks."

"I didn't think so."

I felt an unreasonable urge to start a fight. It was childish and seriously immature, but I itched to grab him, body-slam him, or do something to get his undivided attention...and all his fucking secrets. That last thought hit me like a rogue wave, leaving me sputtering and confused. Again.

"God, I want to kick your ass." I snarled.

Sky looked over at me in surprise and chuckled softly. "I'd love to see you try."

"Hmph. Not worth breaking a fingernail. I don't see what's so hard about being honest."

Sky pursed his lips and set his phone on the table facedown before leaning on his elbows in a deceptively relaxed pose. "Gosh, I didn't realize my life story meant so much to you."

"It doesn't. But your condescending frat boy blow-off is annoying and suspicious as fuck too. I wonder what you're hiding."

"Hiding?"

"Yeah, you heard me. If there's a warrant for your arrest for outstanding traffic violations or a dead body in your freezer, you might as well come clean. Harry might be a softy, but he wouldn't like the cops showing up to handcuff you during business hours. So whatever this fuckin' secret is...spill it now or go find a part-time job somewhere else."

Sky's scathing once-over had a wicked bite. I braced myself for a verbal assault and even shifted in my seat in case he decided to knee me in the balls. But he didn't move, and he didn't speak. He just stared at me for a vampire-length eternity, then slid his elbows forward and raised his brows.

"I'm gay."

Okay. I didn't expect that.

At all.

I narrowed my gaze and cocked my head. "Gay," I repeated.

"Yeah. Gay."

"That's it?"

"Yep. Are you disappointed?"

"Huh? No. It's cool. I don't care if you're gay. I don't think anybody cares anymore," I huffed derisively.

"That's naïve and almost...cute," he said in a patronizing tone. "Lots of people care. My parents cared. They cared a lot."

"Then they suck, and you're better off without them."

He looked away briefly. "Maybe. Doesn't matter. It's done."

I nodded as though I understood what he was saying when of course I had no clue. "So what's their deal? Are they super conservative or just super assholes?"

Sky shrugged. "Both, I guess. My family owns a huge cattle ranch. They have old money and old connections and a gay son doesn't fit the macho cowboy mold. I knew coming out was a risk, but it still sucks to be right."

"Oh." I set my burrito on the wrapper and sipped my drink. I didn't know what to say, but it seemed vaguely important to let him know that while I still thought he was an asshole, it had nothing to do with his gayness. "You're a jerk. Not because you suck cock...I mean—I don't know if you suck cock. Maybe you don't, but—"

"I do," he replied with a mischievous grin. "I'm actually an expert cocksucker."

I swallowed hard and nodded. "Uh...good to know. But for the record, your parents are the real losers. I don't get people who have kids and then turn them away when they dare to be themselves. There ought to be a law against that."

"Yeah. But there's not, so I'm on my own."

"Do you have friends or other family to go to or...?"

"No."

"What about your teammates? Don't they have your back?" I asked persistently. And don't ask me why, 'cause we both probably knew I should have dropped the questions a while ago.

This time when Sky smiled, it didn't quite reach his eyes. "They don't know."

"Oh. Who knows?" I winced automatically and shook my head. "Stupid question. You don't have to tell—"

"No one." He paused for a beat, then added, "Just you."

I pointed at my chest incredulously. "Me? That's it?"

"Well, I guess a couple of other people know, like my ex and his boyfriend...and the ex who came before me. I guess that makes four people total." Sky held my gaze as he bit into his burrito.

"Um...that's cool. But why'd you tell *me*?"

" 'Cause you asked," he deadpanned, reaching for his soda.

"Not really. Okay. Maybe I did, but that wasn't the secret I was expecting."

"It's the only one I got. Unlike you, I don't have a weird hard-on for the Green Lantern."

"Hmph. Well, your secret's safe with me."

"Thanks, but we don't know any of the same people, so it doesn't really matter who you tell."

"That won't be the case if you work for Harry."

"I guess that's true. So, what's the story with Harry anyway?"

"There's no story. He's just the guy who married my mom."

"So you don't like him 'cause he's your stepdad?" Sky asked conversationally.

"I like Harry fine. He's just...*really* nice. Annoyingly nice, if you know what I mean."

"No one knows what you mean."

"Harry's one of those weird people who's never in a bad mood. Ever. He wakes up singing. He smiles at every random person he passes on the street, and he will literally give you the shirt off his back," I groused, shaking my head in disbelief. "He's the guy who buys every gift on a secret Santa wish list or the guy who 'pays it forward' in line at Starbucks. Nice stuff, but sometimes it's overboard. For example, last week in the office, he overheard Sue in accounting tell me that her son's bike got stolen. Harry had a new bike delivered the next day with a big ol' red ribbon."

"Geez, the guy is a certified monster," Sky snarked.

"Well, Sue was pissed," I said, ignoring his sarcasm. "She told her kid every day not to leave his bike outside. And she figured this was a teaching moment. Bikes don't grow on trees, and Santa doesn't make summer appearances. Except he did. And if it was a one-time occurrence, it would be sweet. But according to Sue, Harry already replaced a skateboard and a video game for her other kids this year."

"Hmm. He sounds like a good guy."

"He is. That's why we're having this conversation." I tapped the table obnoxiously. "I don't want you to take advantage of the situation. I probably sound paranoid, but you've rubbed me the wrong way since day one and—why are you lookin' at me like that?"

Sky put his hand over his mouth and snickered. "You feed me so many one-liners, and it's killing me not to use them. Sorry. What were you saying? Something about rubbing the right way...or the wrong way..."

I crossed my arms and sat back in my chair to observe him. I expected a swift return to normal where I'd pick apart all the things I didn't like about this guy and catalog any show of weakness to use against him if necessary. But I had a hard time getting past his twinkling eyes and his wide smile. I looked away quickly before I did something weird, like blush. And why? 'Cause he made a sex joke? That didn't make sense.

I refocused and shook my head ruefully. "As I was saying... Harry's nice, I'm not. And I don't trust you. I don't think I like you either."

"That's okay. I'm used to people not liking me."

"It's not a gay thing, you know," I assured him.

Sky narrowed his eyes. "I didn't say it was."

"Okay. 'Cause I don't care if you're gay, and Harry definitely won't care. He bought a Bi-Pride flag for my best friend when he came out a couple of months ago. To hang in our apartment."

"Did you?"

"Hang the flag? Fuck, no! I told Elliot to put it in his room. It's huge. There's no wall space in there unless he moves his volleyball trophies," I scoffed.

"Hmm. A volleyball player. Is he single?" Sky asked, raising his brows lasciviously.

"No," I replied quickly. "Actually I don't know. He's seeing a guy named Drew now. I haven't met him. I thought I heard them in Elliot's room last night, but maybe he was watching porn. Honestly, I want to get the first meeting over with so we can get past the weirdness."

"Why is it weird?"

I shrugged carelessly. "It's new. He had the same girlfriend for years and...it's something I have to get used to. I don't care if he's bi, but it seemed kinda fast and random. I thought he was kidding at first. I said all the wrong things when he came out, like 'You don't look gay,' and 'Maybe it's a phase.' I even told him he should get it out of his system on the DL and not come out officially for a while."

"Wow. You *are* an asshole."

"I know. I didn't mean to insult him."

"Hmm. What's he look like? Is he hot? Would I like him?"

I furrowed my brow and shot an exasperated look his way. "I don't know what you like, and Elliot is off limits anyway."

"Fine. Is he super tall?"

"Yeah, he's six foot six and thicker than you'd think a volleyball player would be."

"Are we talking about his dick or his biceps now?" Sky asked, popping the last bite of his burrito into his mouth.

"What? Christ! What's the matter with you?" I glanced at our neighboring tables and glared at him. "I am not discussing anyone's dick size with you, asshole."

"We can discuss ass instead," he offered. "Check out that guy next to the door. Very nice rear view."

"You're hilarious." I set my burrito on the wrapper and sucked on my straw, slurping noisily before letting out a belch. I swiped my hand across my mouth. "Why don't we get back to the interview? Here's what I know so far...you're from Idaho, you divorced your wealthy parents, so you're poor now and need a job. Until the scouts come calling."

"Yeah, that pretty much sums up my life. Minus the drama," he added with a self-deprecating shrug that was kind of...cute.

Weird thought because Sky wasn't cute. He was manly, muscular, intense, and model handsome. Looks-wise, he was intimidating as fuck. Not cuddly, adorable, or remotely sweet.

I repeated "Sky's an asshole" in my head a couple of times and did my best not to stare at his mouth when I asked, "Do you think you have a real chance at going pro?"

"A year ago, I would have said yes, but now...I don't know anymore. Do you follow baseball at all?"

"Sure. I'm a Tigers fan."

Sky shot an incredulous look at me. "Only someone from Michigan says that."

"Guilty."

"Oh. Where in Michig—"

"St. Clair Shores, but that's not important. You're the one gettin' grilled here, not me. Who's your team?" I asked.

"Dodgers."

I rolled my eyes. "Everyone loves the fuckin' Dodgers. You're not even from California, and you love 'em."

"I always have. They're probably the number one reason I wanted to move here."

"Oh, brother," I huffed derisively.

"Hey, it's true. I would have moved sooner if I could. I got stuck going to a small private college owned by a friend of the family when I first got out of high school. They had a decent baseball team, but I knew I wouldn't go anywhere unless I transferred. I talked my dad into letting me apply to a few California colleges. I got accepted to UCLA, Fullerton, and Chilton. I wanted to go to Fullerton 'cause they're a Division One baseball powerhouse. But my father was adamant...Chilton or nothing."

"Why?"

"He said it was a better academic school. Maybe so. I didn't care at first. I just wanted out. I figured I'd spend a year at Chilton and transfer to Fullerton or anywhere else. But I met Max and...things changed." Sky popped the lid off and shook the ice before tipping his cup back.

"Who's Max?"

"My ex."

I noted his defiant tone, clenched jaw, and squared shoulders with a vague sense of curiosity. Every time he gave me one measly piece of info, I had twenty more questions. Personal ones. Why did he come out to his parents if he knew it would affect their financial support and possibly lead to outright disinheritance? Especially since he had no plans to come out to anyone else. And what happened between him and Max? In other words, a bunch of shit that was none of my business.

But I couldn't quite let it go.

"Hmph. Let me guess...he gave you an ultimatum to come

out or else. You did and he bounced anyway," I said, crumpling my wrapper in a tiny ball.

"No. Other way around. I told him I wanted to come out. He didn't. I got mad and decided I'd do it myself, starting with my family. It was a disaster. They wanted to commit me."

"To what? A psych ward?"

"Conversion therapy."

"Holy fuck."

"Yeah. I left in the middle of the night, drove back to California, and found Max in bed with his best friend, who happened to be our other roommate...and his ex."

"Whoa."

Sky waved dismissively. "Nah. It's not like that. I knew Max didn't cheat on me. It wasn't his style. He was loyal to a fault. Besides, they were fully clothed. But I still lost my shit. Not immediately. I waited till the next morning. And I unraveled a little more every day. I told Max what went down with my family. I told him I was afraid my dad would come after me while we were at practice and drag me home in a straightjacket. The only way to keep my dignity was to come out on my own terms. I asked Max to come out with me. To make it easier."

"He didn't want to?"

"He wasn't ready," Sky said with a sad-looking half smile. "And I wasn't brave enough to do it on my own. So, I called my dad and told him I made a mistake."

"You went back in the closet?"

"I tried to anyway. I told him I was stressed and not thinking right. Dad agreed that was probably the case. He encouraged me to make some changes in my life...move home and transfer schools before I lost my way to a liberal agenda. Whatever the hell that meant. When he called the athletic director and asked pointed questions about my teammates, I freaked again. I didn't want him probing into anyone's personal business and creating issues. I could just see him popping up on my doorstep to interrogate Max and Christian and...I couldn't do that to them. I figured it was best if I left first."

"What'd you do?"

"I dismantled my life. I quit the team, moved out of the apartment, and broke up with Max. Then I went home. And guess who was waiting for me?"

"A conversion therapist."

"No, a priest. But I figured the therapist was next, so I left again. I drove to California, crashed on friend's sofa, and went into full panic mode when my dad demanded I return immediately, see the specialists he chose, and re-enroll at St. John's. Basically give him control of my life until I proved myself capable. And reliable enough that he wouldn't have to worry about me dragging our family name through the mud by doing something stupid like getting caught dirty dancing in a gay club." He snorted and shook his head.

"Do you dirty dance in gay clubs?" I widened my eyes comically, hoping to lighten the mood.

Sky shot a wicked grin at me. "Every chance I get. And you wanna know why?"

"Uh, sure."

" 'Cause I'm not a little bit gay. I'm *really* fucking gay."

"Good to know."

"And I didn't want to move home, give up baseball, and get a pretend girlfriend to please my parents. Geez, I don't think I could get hard if I rubbed against a hot naked girl to save my life. I'm not wired that way."

"So what did you tell your parents?"

"I told them I was staying in Cali." Sky tipped his cup again and chomped on a mouthful of ice obnoxiously.

He kept his eyes locked on mine as though daring me to judge him. The dude was so damn prickly. Deceptively cool and calm one second and ready to rip my throat out the next. On some level, I always seemed to connect with weirdos like him. Hell, that pretty much described every guy on my team. Except none of them made my heart race and my dick twitch.

I tore my gaze from his mouth and inclined my head. "Okay. Um…good. I'm not sure what that has to do with accounting, but—"

"You wanted my life story, and you got it. You brought up Harry, then your bi roommate because the queer stuff is bugging you."

"It doesn't bug me."

"All right. It confuses you and probably has you wondering why it feels heavy."

I frowned so hard, I gave myself a headache. "What the fuck is that supposed to mean?"

Sky fixed me with a fierce expression. "Whatever you think it means. Maybe it's too much information at once. Or maybe it's weird for you to change your perception of your friend. Or… maybe you can relate. And you don't want to."

"How?"

He shrugged with faux indifference. "Maybe you're gay or bi…and very much in the closet. Like me."

Blood rushed from my face so fast, I thought I might pass out. My mouth went dry and my heart raced and if I was confused before, I was flat-out lost now. Nothing made sense. I shouldn't be here with Sky, sharing personal things, and he shouldn't think we had anything in common. Because we didn't.

But if he got it all wrong, none of this should make me sweat. And it did.

I licked my dry lips as I rested my elbows on the table, careful not to brush against his arm. "No. That's not—I'm not… wh-why…what makes you think that?"

Sky cocked his head and observed me like an odd specimen

under a microscope. "C'mon, Colby. Why are we here? Be honest. I've seen the way you look at me."

"Like you're an asshole?"

"Maybe I am. But if we'd met in a club instead of an econ class, I have a feeling we'd have blown each other a long time ago," he singsonged.

I stared at his mouth for a moment too long before I caught the ready humor in his eyes and realized he was joking. *Right. Okay.* Which meant it was my turn to come up with something witty or snarky. I came up blank. Worse...I couldn't stop wondering what it would feel like to have him suck my cock. He seemed like the kind of person who excelled at everything he tried. No doubt he was a pro. He'd know how much pressure to apply and when to angle his head and when to swallow and *—oh, fuck.*

"Yeah, right," I huffed. I crumbled the mess of napkins with the remains of my lunch into a ball and stood. "Well, this has been fun, but I'm out."

Sky pushed his chair from the table. He tossed his trash into the bin and waited for me to join him on the sidewalk outside.

"I'll see you Monday. And don't worry, I got this...no cooking the books or funneling money to the Caymans," he said as he slipped his sunglasses on his nose.

"Just crunch the fuckin' numbers, and stay out of trouble. Later." I pulled my keys from my pocket and headed for my car.

"Wait up."

I didn't. I needed to get away from him asap. My body wasn't cooperating with my brain, and the last thing I wanted was for Sky to think I liked him. I could put up with him for a few days of training, but I didn't want a new friend. Not Sky, anyway. I unlocked the door and reached for the handle just as he yanked my T-shirt.

"What do you want?"

He pulled his sunglasses off and let out a deep breath. "You know, I was kidding back there. I'm sorry if I came on too strong."

"You mean you don't want to suck my dick?" I crossed my arms and leaned against the car door.

"Oh, no, I'd totally suck your dick. I probably shouldn't have said it out loud. That's all."

"Probably not." I noticed the slight tug of a smile at the corner of Sky's mouth. "What's so damn funny?"

"Nothing. You're an interesting combination of a hard-ass thug and a nice guy. It's kinda sweet."

"You're calling me a sweet thug?" I asked with a laugh. "Do you *want* your ass kicked?"

Sky grinned and motioned for me to take a swing. "Do it. Hit me with your best shot. Just not in the face."

He danced toward me and jabbed my bicep, then hopped out of reach and did it again.

"What are you doing?"

I reached for his hand just as he grabbed my wrists and backed me against my Prius. There wasn't much room to maneuver in the confined space between my car and the Suburban next to it, and he was too quick anyway. Sky stepped between my legs, so close I could smell the sun on his skin and feel his dick and—*oh, my God.*

I sucked in a breath and swallowed around the Sahara in my mouth. His gaze flitted from my lips to my eyes. It was like that day in the classroom. The heat, the energy, the sizzling sense of awareness. Only this time we were in public. Sort of. No one could see us. We were sheltered by a wall on one side and an SUV on the other, but I could hear traffic and laughter in the distance. I should have pushed him away. I knew he'd back off. I had free will and plenty of muscle. I could have turned this around in a flash. But I wanted to see what he'd do next.

He didn't do anything.

Sky let go of my wrists and stepped away. And fuck, that was worse.

I bit my bottom lip and did my best to get my heart rate under control. But my pulse was racing, my head was spinning, and there was only one way to make everything stop. I grabbed a fistful of Sky's T-shirt, yanked him to my chest, and crashed my mouth over his.

Okay, let me explain something here...I'd never kissed a guy or been kissed by a guy in my life. Ever. I'd thought about it a couple of times, but I never let the idea become anything more than a passing curiosity, 'cause kissing another man was gay, and I wasn't gay.

But I must have been kind of gay, because I liked this. A lot.

I liked the contrast of his stubbled jaw and soft lips. I liked the sexy sound he made when he licked the seam of my mouth and pushed his tongue between my lips. I didn't like Diet Coke, but I didn't mind the taste of it on him. And fuck, he smelled good too. Like some kind of woodsy cologne and expensive soap. And it got even better when he tilted his hips slightly so his erection pressed against mine.

I didn't want him to stop. There was a "rightness" in the slide of his tongue, the roll of his hips, and the feel of his hands on my waist. It didn't make sense, but I swore something inside me shifted and settled, and nothing about this seemed wrong. I wanted more. I didn't know how to ask for it, so I let him lead, grateful when he angled his head and deepened the connection.

Sky sucked my bottom lip, then licked it, slipping his hand under my T-shirt and flattening it on my lower back as our tongues twisted in a growing frenzy. I lost track of time. Maybe a minute passed. Maybe twenty. I was locked into the moment in a way I only ever experienced when I was on the ice. I lost myself in the push and pull of unfamiliar sensation. His cock was so damn hard. Or was that me?

I lowered my hand to adjust myself and accidentally grabbed Sky's junk instead. Well, okay...it wasn't an accident. He rocked forward and I didn't pull away. We were in the middle of a major lip-lock, so it was a perfectly logical progression. But I freaked. I let go and pushed his chest. Hard.

He stumbled back a step, raising his hands in self-defense as I swiped my forearm across my mouth and panted like I'd just run a marathon.

"I'm not...I don't want..." I whispered.

Sky nodded slowly. "Shh. It's okay."

"It's not okay. You kissed me." I heaved a sigh and stared at a couple of crows squawking on a telephone wire above us.

"No, *you* kissed me," he corrected. When I didn't reply, he looked up at the birds, then stepped closer. "Hey, don't freak out. It's just us here."

I met his gaze and let out a ragged rush of air. "I don't want to do that again."

"Okay. We won't. We'll pretend it didn't happen."

"Okay."

Sky pursed his lips thoughtfully before inclining his head. "I'll see you Monday."

I watched him walk away, then opened the car door and sank into the driver's seat. I turned the engine on, glanced in the rearview mirror, and curled my fingers around the gearshift. My right hand shook so bad, I couldn't get it to move. I left it in park and sucked in a deep breath. And another. A rap song blared through the speakers. Something slightly obscene that I recognized from team parties where we'd stand around a beer keg cradling red Solo cups and making idle conversation with adoring hockey groupies. You know, girls who showed up to every game and treated us like fuckin' rock stars. If it had been any other normal day, I would have sung along to a line or two, changed the station, and been on my way.

But this wasn't a normal day.

I killed the engine and pulled the key from the ignition, letting the silence roll over me. *Holy fuck.* What just happened? I'd been doing so well. I'd avoided him for weeks. No eye contact, no interaction whatsoever. Yeah, he chased me down to drop the job bomb, but I could have put an end to it immediately. I could have nodded, made an excuse to get away, and told Harry that Sky was a bad bet.

But I ate lunch with him instead. And kissed him. The burrito sat in my stomach like a lead balloon. I felt slightly nauseous yet tingly all over at the same time. I wanted to get as far from Sky Jameson as possible. But first I wanted to rewind the last ten minutes of my life and play them over again.

And yeah...that scared the hell out of me.

3

The best cure for a panic attack on deck was a trip to the rink. Team practices started next week, which meant the bulk of the guys were out of town soaking up the last bit of summer vacation while they had a chance. I hoped it also meant I wouldn't run into anyone I knew. At least no one who'd want to chat about anything that required extra brain cells. Sure, I wished I had pads, a stick, and a reason to body-slam someone as I chased after a puck. But organizing a pick-up game was too much work and required talking. I couldn't do that without cracking or acting weird.

I tried to be as "normal" as possible. I shot the shit with the guy manning the reception desk about sharing ice time with figure skaters, the Kings' chances next season, and the heat wave happening beyond the air-conditioned walls. Then I strapped on my skates, popped my earpods in, and skated. And skated. And skated.

I cut across the ice at top speeds, taking the corners at wicked angles while listening to mind-numbing metal rock. I hoped the rush of adrenaline would eventually erase the memory of that kiss...and the feel of his body against mine. Lap after lap, I zipped along the perimeter, wiping sweat from my brow in some oddball attempt to out-skate an invisible demon. My legs were rubbery, and my thighs burned. The familiar aches and pains were reassuring. But they didn't stop the replay button in my head. Sky's hand on my hip, his warm skin and firm grip. *Holy fuck.* I crouched low and picked up my pace in a last-ditch effort to outrun him so I could breathe again.

But the suffocating feeling didn't go away. It followed me to the gym and stuck with me as I pumped weights, then beat the crap out of the punching bag. It receded enough that I was hopeful I'd avoided a full-blown meltdown by the time I pushed the door open to the two-bedroom apartment I shared with Elliot.

Our place was small, and the walls were super thin. No joke. If Elliot farted in his bedroom, I could hear it in the kitchen. The living room and kitchen were divided by a mini island with two pendant lights above it. I appreciated not having wasted space, like a dining room that never got used, but I wished the bedrooms were larger and that we had our own bathrooms. Elliot's interior designer mom arranged the hand-me-down furniture we inherited from my mom and Harry into something vaguely chic. The color scheme was a basic nautical. Her description, not ours. A denim sectional sofa and surfboard-style coffee table faced a giant flat-screen. Two beanbag chairs provided extra seating when we had friends over to hang out and watch movies or just play video games.

I dropped my bag in the entry and peeled off my damp T-shirt before glancing around for signs of life. I could usually tell when Elliot was home. He tended to spread himself around like a dog marking his territory. He'd shuck off his shoes at the door, leave his keys on the island, and his backpack on the sofa. If it was a cold day, his jacket would be draped over a barstool or lying on the floor. I loved the guy, but I was grateful to be alone.

My goal was to shower, scrounge for food, then hibernate in my room till morning.

I headed for the bathroom at the end of the hall and turned on the water, studiously avoiding my reflection as I finished undressing. I was just about to step under the spray when I heard a thump. I frowned and went still.

Thump, thump, thump.

It sounded like Morse code or like someone was trying to escape from a closet. What could I say? True crime shows were my jam. I pulled a towel around my waist and went to investigate. I left the shower running 'cause it took forever for the water to get warm. I figured it would be ready by the time I checked my room and Elliot's...you know, just to be sure everything was safe and sound.

I scanned my bedroom quickly, noting my inexpertly made bed, the laptop computer on my desk under the window, and the empty laundry basket next to my closet. Nothing out of place, I mused before moving toward Elliot's room. And there it was again.

Thump, thump, thump... "Oh, fuck. Yeah, that's good."

Oh.

I froze outside the closed door and listened to the telltale sounds of sex in progress. Bedsprings squeaking, skin slapping, and erotic grunts peppered with a steady stream of "Oh fuck, yes." And yes, two male voices.

I didn't know enough about gay sex to know what was happening, but my imagination filled in the blanks. I stared at the door until the steady thump of a headboard hitting the wall escalated a couple of notches.

"Yeah, right there. More. Fuck, I'm close," someone who wasn't Elliot grunted.

I backed away from the door quickly and hurried to the bathroom. I grabbed a towel from the hook behind me and wiped the steam from the mirror. My eyes were wild, my skin looked blotchy, and my dick stuck out like a fucking flagpole. I held on to the faux-marble counter and stroked myself as a kaleidoscope of sexy images flooded my brain...all featuring Sky. Sky on his knees, his lips wrapped around my shaft, his tongue twirling lazy circles around the head of my cock. Sky swallowing me whole.

I squeezed my eyes shut and let my hips fly. Every fantasy fueled by that kiss in the parking lot bubbled to the surface, demanding immediate attention. I could tell myself it didn't matter later. I could tell myself I was just curious. I could tell myself no one would care. But right now, I needed release.

I cupped my balls as I upped the tempo, letting my imagination go one step further. What would Sky do if I told him I was close? Would he swallow or tell me to fuck him? I had no idea how to fuck a guy, but I'd figure it out. I'd push my cock in his tight hole and—*bam!* My orgasm hit me like a freight train. Cum shot over my fingers and splattered the countertop. I squeezed my eyes shut and gasped for air.

When I felt like I could stand without stumbling, I stepped back and surveyed the damage. The bathroom looked like a sauna and smelled like cum. I used the towel to wipe the counter, tossed it on the floor, and jumped into the shower. I stood under the warm spray and hung my head, letting the water sluice over my skin and wash away the evidence. And maybe I hoped it washed something inside of me too. I didn't want this...whatever this was. I just wanted to be me.

I took the fastest shower possible, pulled a clean towel from Elliot's stash on the shelf over the toilet, and dried off before wrapping it around my waist. I listened for signs of life, then hurried to my room to get dressed and get out.

I called Troy and Logan and asked them to meet up for pizza. We hung out at the food court near campus, talking sports, our team's chances next season, and our class loads in the fall semester. General topics that kept my mind from spinning. I must have done a decent job of acting normal, 'cause they didn't seem suspicious or ask any probing questions. We didn't have practice the next day, but they reminded me about Schultz's party Saturday night. They might have even mentioned hot babes, booze, and a good chance to get laid. I just nodded absently and waved good-bye.

But I still didn't go home. I moved on to my favorite comic shop and sat in a corner, reading old Avengers comics until closing time. I told myself I wanted to give Elliot space, but the truth was…I was freaked out. Majorly freaked out.

I'm bi.

Maybe I'd always known and didn't want to deal with it. Maybe I hoped it was an "out of sight, out of mind" thing. It wasn't. It was real. It wasn't going away. I didn't want to go to parties with babes and booze. I wanted things I didn't think I could talk about. 'Cause I wasn't ready to say that word out loud. Not even to Elliot. I needed time to get used to the idea that I might not be who I thought I was.

EITHER ELLIOT DIDN'T KNOW I'd overheard him and his new guy, or he chose to ignore it. The following morning, he gave me a fist bump, scratched his balls through his boxer briefs, then poured himself a cup of coffee like he did every other day. I grunted a greeting as I observed him over the rim of my mug. Elliot was huge. He was six foot six with broad shoulders, a trim waist, and a mop of shaggy light-brown hair. He was a quintessential California beach bum in the best possible way. People gravitated to Elliot. He had a friendly demeanor and a cool but kind vibe that made him seem approachable. And usually, the guy was an open book.

He was quiet this morning. Of course, he did just wake up, I mused as I glanced toward the bedroom and listened for the sound of someone rustling around. Nothing. And he only took out one cup. But maybe his friend didn't drink coffee. *Hmm. Sociopath.*

"You got home late. What'd you do last night?" Elliot asked, leaning against the island.

"The usual. No big deal."

"Hmm. You look funny. Like you got some." He waggled his eyebrows lasciviously.

"Nope." I waited a beat and asked, "Did you?"

He chuckled when I mimicked his eyebrow gesture, then smiled and changed the subject. "We're supposed to be at the beach before eleven. And don't try to get out of it. You promised to play. Tucker is going down early 'cause he's type-A about the net. He's not wrong. Most of them need to be replaced or..."

That was it. Awkward conversation averted. He rambled on about the sorry condition of the volleyball nets at the beach like he was collecting information to report to the parks and rec department. Or like he thought I gave a crap when all I really wanted to know was if he fucked a guy in his room last night. And I wanted details. What was it like? How did it feel? Things I'd never ask but kinda sorta really wanted to know.

And yeah, he should know he could talk to me about guys too. I could have reassured him that it was cool by me. If I was feeling brave, I could tell him about me too. But I wasn't brave. I was freaked out. So I kept quiet, sipped my coffee, and told myself not to rush. Maybe I really was just going through a phase. And maybe it would be over by Monday.

My friends talked me into going to Schultz's party. I didn't want to go. At all. First of all, Jason Schultz was a douche. Secondly, his idea of a "party" was more of a "gathering of his admirers." And the guy loved the hockey rock-god attention. Don't get me wrong, I didn't mind retelling my version of an awesome goal or a crazy mid-game brawl on the ice, but it made for lopsided conversations with me doing all the talking. And honestly, I didn't like talking about myself that much.

I spent most of the night leaning against a wall in the kitchen, nursing a beer and planning my escape. I had my opening when someone bumped into the cute blonde who'd been glued to my side all night. I set my empty bottle on the crowded countertop and glanced over her shoulder at a pretty brunette with glasses. She stopped short and pointed at my chest.

"Oh, my—I know you. Colby from econ. How'd you do on the final?" she asked, flipping her long hair over her shoulder.

"Pretty good. You?"

"Aced it," Miss Smartypants bragged, holding her hand up for a high five.

I touched my palm to hers, dodging a few partygoers making their way into the kitchen so I could hear her over the din of the music. The girl I'd been talking to disappeared in the melee, leaving me with the chatty brainiac. I nodded as she went on about grade point averages and grad school. I spotted Troy and Logan in the living room, surrounded by a posse of admirers. They loved the attention. I doubted they'd notice if I left, I mused, gauging the distance between the kitchen and the front door. I refocused on Miss Smartypants when I sensed a change in her cadence.

"—you know him, right?"

"Who?"

"Jason. Of course, you do. He's on your team. Do you know if he's single?" she asked, shooting a longing look toward Schultz, who was standing near the sliding glass door.

"I think so. I dunno. Why? Are you interested in him?"

"Maybe." She bit her bottom lip and gave me a shy look that didn't quite go with her usual uber-confident attitude.

"Do you want me to introduce you or something?"

"Yeah, but don't be obvious." She clutched at my arm and squealed. "Oh my God, he's coming over. Pretend we're hanging out and act cool."

I furrowed my brow in confusion, then jolted when someone smacked my back hard from behind.

"Hey, Fish! How's it going, man? Glad you could make it," Schultz enthused.

"It's a team party, why wouldn't I come?"

Schultz shrugged. "I dunno. I thought maybe you were a little...you know, jealous."

I shot an amused smile his way and shook my head. "Nope. I'm happy for you." *Asshole.*

"Thanks. It's been intense. I could barely walk after practice yesterday and..."

I zoned out while Schultz bragged about his first couple of days with the Kings. I was aware of Miss Smartypants next to me, hanging on his every word, and a few others in the vicinity tuning into hear about his initial brush with greatness. In the midst of planning round three of my great escape, I couldn't help noticing Schultz sizing up Miss Smartypants. I knew that look. If he thought she was with me, he'd lay on a little extra charm just to prove he could have whatever and whoever he wanted. But he didn't stop to introduce himself to her or give me a chance to do the honors. Which reminded me, I still didn't know her name.

"That's awesome," I interrupted somewhere in the middle of his gory tale about the size of the new blister on his ankle. I put my arm around Miss Smartypants's shoulders to keep her close when someone barreled by us, dripping beer from a Solo cup. "Hey, I want you to meet my frie—"

"I'm Kendra," she supplied, holding her hand out like royalty.

Schultz glanced at her outstretched hand in amusement, then at me. The lapse in time was just long enough to be rude, and something in me snapped. I laced my fingers with hers, kissed her knuckles, and inclined my head toward the living area.

"C'mon babe, I want to introduce you to someone else." I nodded an absent good-bye at Schultz and led her into the living area.

She batted me away when we reached a corner near the window. "What did you just do?"

"He's a dick. You can do better than him," I said.

"I don't want to marry him, dummy!"

I threw my hands in the air and snorted. "Good. But you can arrange your own booty call. I don't want any part of that. And I'm the world's worst wingman anyway."

"You are," she agreed with a huff. "You called me 'babe.' Now everyone is going to think we're together."

"I'm sorry. That was weird of me. But seriously, there are a lot of other nice guys on my team. My friend Troy is cool. Want to meet him? I'll introduce you before I leave and—"

"You can't leave me here. People will think we broke up."

I frowned. "We aren't together."

"Yeah, but you just announced that we are, so now you're stuck with me for a little while."

I fixed her with a fierce stare. "I'm staying for ten minutes, tops."

"Twenty."

"Fifteen," I countered.

"Deal."

I chuckled when she held out her hand, but I shook it like a gentleman, then steered her toward a couple of eligible bachelors who I knew for a fact were decent guys.

WE HUNG out together for another hour before I finally convinced her I had to go home. But I had to admit, it was kind of fun. No doubt my friends would have a million questions about my surprise new girlfriend at practice next week. Kendra didn't look or act like any of the other girls: she didn't wear much makeup, her dress was cute but not particularly sexy, and she pushed her glasses up on her nose every few minutes. I couldn't help feeling a little protective of her; she was a like a minnow swimming in a shark tank. She was quirky as hell, but she was pleasant company. And a nice respite from obsessing over Sky.

Until she mentioned him out of the fucking blue as I walked her to her car.

"Sky?"

"Yeah, the smokin' hot guy from econ. You remember him, don't you? He always sat by the window. Blondish hair, blue eyes, a body that—"

"Yeah, yeah, yeah. I remember. What about him?" I asked gruffly.

"Do you have his number?" She pointed her key fob at a Hyundai like she was holding a loaded gun, then spun around and handed me her cell. "You should give me yours too. Now that your friends kind of think we're dating, it would seem strange if I didn't know how to contact you. Feel free to add Sky's too."

"What's with you? You seem like you're on a mission to...you know."

"I am. I'm twenty-two and I've never done anything...fun. I made a promise to myself that I would do *everything* before I graduate. The clock is ticking." Kendra tapped her wrist for emphasis. "No more waiting on the sidelines. I'm not going to be shy anymore. I'm going after what I want."

I typed in my number, returned her cell, and slipped my hands in my pockets. "Good for you. But you're on your own. I told you, I'm not your wingman."

"That's fine. You can be my friend." She beamed.

I smiled. "Sounds good."

BAILEY, Barnes, and Cohen was located in a Spanish-style building in Belmont Shores a block away from the beach. The prime location, friendly partners, and generous perks made BBC a cool place to work. If you wanted to be an accountant. And I did not...I repeat, did *not* want to be an accountant. Nothing against the profession. I loved numbers, and I probably had what it took to be a great CPA. I was diligent, concise, and spreadsheets kinda turned me on. But I didn't want to work for Harry. I already owed him enough. I was grateful for sure, but I was ready to do my own thing.

I slapped a high five with Meg, the receptionist on duty, and inclined my head toward the curtain of silver streamers dividing the upscale wood-and-marble accented lobby area from the main office.

"Whose birthday is it?"

"Chandra, Karen, and Willy's. You missed it. We sang at lunch," she said with a wink, tucking a strand of her long black curly hair behind her ear. Meg was a pretty, petite African American woman with a fun sense of humor and a quick wit. She'd been working for Harry for years. Maybe decades. She might make fun of his silly traditions, but she was fiercely loyal to him.

"Oh, darn," I deadpanned.

"Lucky you. I saved you some ice cream cake. Mint chip and chocolate. You're welcome."

"Thanks."

"No problem. The new intern is here. Harry gave him the grand tour and introduced him around. They're either in Harry's office or at your desk. And can I just say…holy smokes!" Meg batted her eyelashes and giggled like a schoolgirl.

It was kind of funny to see someone my mom's age go gaga over a guy. But I understood. And somehow, I had to play it cool and get through the next three hours without doing anything weird. Like staring at him or getting hard if Sky sat too close.

"Good to know," I huffed, rolling my eyes before parting the curtain of streamers and moving through the maze of cubicles on the other side.

I paused to give a fist bump or two on my way to my desk, located in a blessedly quiet section next to the copy room. It was the office space no one wanted because it was like an island… nowhere near the kitchen, conference rooms, or the restrooms. And there were no windows. Not an issue for a part-time employee who generally got pulled into partners' offices to help on various projects. I set my computer bag on my desk and was about to pull out my chair when I heard Harry's booming voice nearby.

"Has anyone seen Colby?"

I groaned inwardly, then squared my shoulders and skirted the partition to greet my stepdad and the new hire. I spotted Sky's head above the cubicles before Harry and he came into view. "Hey, Harry. I'm here."

Harry flashed a bright smile and motioned for Sky to follow him.

Harry Cohen was a roly-poly oddball who loved to laugh. Physically, there was nothing extraordinary about him. He was short, round, and bald. His trademark hairy dark eyebrows looked vaguely like caterpillars resting on his brow. They took on a life of their own, waggling expressively whenever he got excited.

And everything excited Harry. His eyes twinkled as he went into a spiel about how happy he was to have Sky join the BBC team that was so damn sincere, anyone would think Sky was an accounting guru with years of experience instead of a lowly part-time intern.

I nodded in Harry's general direction, but Sky had my complete attention. He looked...good. Really good. He wore a pair of fitted khakis and a blue button-down shirt. Nothing exciting, but I noticed this summer when he wore shorts and plain T-shirts that everyday clothes looked better on him than normal people.

"How's it going, Sky?" I asked, extending my hand.

The instant zing of awareness shot through my fingertips, up my arms, and through my chest. And when Sky squeezed my hand more firmly than necessary, I knew he felt it too.

"Good. Nice to see you again," he replied politely. "I was just telling Harry about our lunch the other day."

I arched my brow. "Oh, really?"

"Glad to hear you two have become good friends," Harry chortled, patting me on the back. "We'll have you over for dinner sometime, Sky."

"Uh...sure. That would be nice," he said, shooting a sideways glance at me.

"Great, great! We'll pick a night Colby's free too. In the meantime, I'll let you two get to work. First order of business...help Sky get acquainted with the system, Colb. You can ease him in with the McGregor files. Poor guy has been busy with HR paperwork all morning. I'm sure he's more than ready to get to the good stuff."

Not rolling my eyes was freaking killing me. I gave myself a gold star and nodded.

"Cool. Follow me. We'll have more space to work in the conference room." I pointed at the glass fishbowl on the far side of the space.

"Why not use Bailey's office?" Harry suggested. "He's in Europe with his family for the next two weeks. It's big enough to stretch out, and it's quieter on that side of the building."

"Um...sure. We can do that." I smiled at Harry, then grabbed my BBC laptop before motioning for Sky to follow me. "This way."

Ron Bailey and Chester Barnes's offices were separated by a long corridor and a quaint atrium-slash-lobby that employees used to have a cup of coffee or read. It was a designated quiet space. The kitchen and outdoor seating area were social spaces, I explained as I steered him toward the large corner office.

Sky made a beeline for the window and gazed at the view of the Pacific Ocean while I rattled off a few lame office rules that HR had probably already gone over.

"This is nice. Accountants must do well in this neighborhood," Sky commented, sliding a chair behind the enormous wood desk and sitting next to me.

"Bailey and Barnes do wealth management, and Cohen is the accountant. Doesn't sound as fancy, but Harry manages everyone. I've seen the books. He makes more money than B and B combined, but he keeps it on the DL and smiles all the way to the bank." I opened my laptop and typed my password, then gestured toward the cup of pens and the pad of paper beside it. "You're gonna wanna take notes. We can probably get through most of the basics in a couple of hours, so you can handle a few reports on your own. If you have any questions, save them for me. I wouldn't ask Harry even though he'll offer. Trust me, it'll add an hour to your day. All right. You ready?"

Sky scooted his chair closer still and tapped a pen on the notepad. "Yep."

I spent the next thirty minutes giving him a brief tutorial of the software program we used and showing off a few bells and whistles before opening the McGregor file. "Okay. This is a BBC computer specifically issued to me. Did they say when you'll be getting yours?"

"Tomorrow."

"Cool. It'll be configured like this one." I pointed at the icons for the programs I'd discussed, then gave him a sideways glance. "I'd suggest not downloading any porn. Save that for your own computer."

"Thanks for the warning. Is that something you learned the hard way?"

Was it my imagination, or did Sky put a little extra emphasis on the word "hard" as he pressed his thigh against mine? Not that it mattered because the second the thought crossed my mind, my dick swelled in my jeans. *Fuck me.* And I'd been doing so well. I'd been all business, one hundred percent serious and focused. And now...I had to think of something intelligent to say.

"You smell good," I blurted.

Fail. As in...*wow.* Total fail.

"Thanks. So do you."

I shook my head as I turned to face him. "Sorry. I didn't mean it that way."

"What way?"

"A gay way. I meant...you smell better than you did last time," I said in a rush.

He chuckled. "Oh?"

"Yeah, um...you smelled like sunshine. But like sweaty

sunshine." Not good, but it was all I had. I stared at the computer screen until my certain blush faded.

Sky pressed his thigh against mine again and sniffed my shirt. "You smell like soap and maybe a little cologne."

I shifted in my chair and huffed sarcastically. "I don't wear cologne."

"Your soap must be perfumed or something."

"The fuck?" I shoved away from the desk and wheeled back to put some space between us. I'd officially reached my limit. I couldn't be this close to him and not combust. And yeah, that was probably super fucking gay, but I couldn't worry about that right now. It was more important that I didn't come in my jeans.

"What kind do you use? Let me guess. You like green, so... Irish Spring?" he asked, not bothering to hide his smile.

"No." I pushed his chair so it rolled a few inches. "What makes you think I like the color green?"

"Green Lantern, of course. And you're wearing a green shirt." He scooted close again and tugged my sleeve.

I furrowed my brow in mock indignation. "This is bluish gray. Not green. And I don't have a thing for Green Lantern, so—"

"You said you did."

"No, I didn't."

"Did too."

"Did fucking not. And if you don't quit throwing my words at me, I'm gonna..."

"You're gonna what?" he prodded.

I stared at his full lips for a long moment and gulped when I felt a pull in his direction. Like he was a magnet. If I got too close, I'd end up doing something I shouldn't. Again.

"Nothing." I hooked my thumb at my laptop. "Let's get back to this."

"Okay." He inclined his head and shrugged. "Must be a secret soap."

"Dude, I use Dove or Ivory or something boring like that. No scent." I sniffed my arm like that was proof before typing gibberish on my keyboard to look busy.

"Got it. Green is not your favorite color, and you never watch porn."

"No green, yes porn."

Sky's eyes twinkled merrily. "But not in the office."

"No way. With my luck, Harry'd sneak up behind me just as the tits.com browser popped up. He'd probably comment on her beautiful hair and lovely tattoos while I pressed 'exit' and wondered if I'd ever get an erection again."

Sky threw his head back and guffawed. "Poor guy would have a heart attack if he saw my browser history."

"Dicks.com, eh?"

"Yep. A few variations, but that's the general theme."

I kept my fingers on the keyboard and typed, "llsyayioqiei-ieooplnkfaeflje…" I couldn't look at him and talk about dick or porn or soap or my favorite color without stuttering. The longer I sat next to him, the harder it was to act cool and collected and business-y. But I couldn't deny I was curious too. Between that kiss last week in the parking lot and Elliot's booty call, my mind had wandered to new places. I had so many questions. The type I should probably have saved for Google. Sky was less than a foot away, though. And I couldn't help remembering how sweet he tasted and how damn good he felt.

I lifted my hands from the keys and licked my lips before turning to him. "When did you know you were gay?"

Sky arched a brow and crossed his arms. "I think I was twelve. Why?"

I ignored his question and barreled on. "How'd you know? Was it one day or a lot of days put together? Hey, I know this is out of the blue and unprofessional. And in spite of what you're thinking, this isn't about me. I'm just...curious."

Sky didn't reply right away. He stared at me like he was waiting for me to crack and admit to my dick having a heartbeat of its own since he sat beside me. When I didn't flinch, he smiled gently and leaned forward. "Who is it about?"

"I overheard my roommate and his new...dude...doin' it."

"Doing what?"

"It," I said sharply.

"Okay. But what exactly did you hear?"

"Everything. Squeaky bedsprings, a thumping noise, and sex grunts. Like 'oh, yeah,' 'right there.' That kinda thing."

"They were fucking," he deadpanned.

"That's what I said!" I pushed my hand through my hair in agitation. "I don't have a problem with it at all, but..."

"Obviously you do. Are you jealous?"

"Why would I be jealous?"

"Because you have a secret crush on your roommate," he offered with a shrug.

My "What the fuck?" expression must have registered loud and clear, because he raised his hands in surrender a moment later and busted up laughing.

"First of all, no fucking way. Elliot and I are best friends. I'm not attracted to him, and I'm definitely not jealous. I'm freaking out because I can't stop thinking about..."

"About what?" he prodded gently.

I caught myself before I said "you." Phew. I fixated on a palm tree swaying in the breeze outside for a second, then let out a nervous half laugh. "No. It's nothing. Never mind. Sorry. Let's get back to McGregor's file. This is a family-owned business. They have storage facilities up and down the coa—"

"Not so fast." Sky set his hand on my elbow and waited for

me to face him before continuing, "You can ask me anything, but what are you freaked out about?"

"I don't know, I just...have questions."

"Keep going..." He made a circular motion with his hands, wordlessly telling me to spit it out.

"How does it work? Who does what? How does it feel? You know...sex questions," I whisper-hissed.

"You need to get on the internet. Google 'gay sex.' "

I pushed my computer aside protectively. "No way."

"Relax. Sex is fun. Don't let it scare you. Can I just say...Sex-Ed day one? I think I'm gonna like this place." Sky pulled his cell from his pocket and set it on the desk. "The doctor is in. Ask a question, any question. Wait. You already did. How do you do it? Simple. Dick in ass. That's it."

"Thanks, I know what anal sex is."

"Good. It sounds like you heard your roommate fucking his boyfriend or vice versa. No cause for alarm. People do it all the damn time and I assure you, with the right partner, it feels fucking amazing."

"So, you've...um"—I narrowed my eyes and scratched my stubbled jaw—"done that?"

Sky cocked his head and gave me one of those slow-growing, wicked grins that should have bugged the hell out of me. But all I could think was, *I want to kiss him again.*

"Yeah, I've done that. A lot. But not much recently. I'm going through a dry spell."

I gulped. "Um...that's—me too. I haven't done the gay stuff, but—"

"But you want to," he said matter-of-factly.

Suddenly, almost all the blood in my body was now in my dick. I'd never been so hard or horny and so completely out of my element at the same time. Ever. I liked the way he smelled and smiled and the feel of his body close to mine.

"You wish," I huffed like a lame-ass.

Sky smiled. Then he rolled his chair away a few inches and leaned back. "Listen, if you really just want to know how to talk to your friend, my advice is...don't act any different. If your brain is working too hard to figure out the mechanics of what he might be doing behind a closed door, that's on you."

"What do you mean?"

"It's private. If he wanted you to see, he would have left the door open. Or fucked him on the sofa. I've done that before."

"You have?"

"Yeah. Our roommate walked in on Max and me and...it wasn't my finest moment." Sky waved dismissively. "Look, if you have the kind of friendship where you can ask personal questions without getting fidgety and weird, do it. If not, do a little research on your own. Look it up."

"Huh? Look up what?"

"Gay sex."

I held both hands up like a traffic guard. "Whoa. I'm not doin' that."

Sky chuckled as he reached for his cell. He typed something, then handed it over to me. "Press Enter. The Google entry is pretty tame. Just two guys kissing or lying in bed. Not porn."

"No way."

"Oh, please. You kissed me in the parking lot last week. Don't tell me you didn't jerk off when you heard your roommate boning his friend. I wasn't even there, and I think it's hot. I would have jerked off for sure."

"Shut up, Jameson," I growled, pushing his phone toward him.

"If you didn't want to talk about it, you wouldn't have brought it up. Be honest. You've probably been thinking about this for months, and now everything is coming at you in stereo. Your roommate, me...it's only natural you'd be a little curious."

I tapped the screen as I tossed his cell on the desk. If naked guys getting it on popped up, I could claim it was an accident. Genius, right? Except the password alert lit up instead. I shrugged nonchalantly and started to turn to the computer just as Sky typed in a code, hit Enter and...*boom!* I couldn't not look.

Not that there was much to see. Two guys lying on a bed and kissing. Implied nudity, but nothing graphic. There were maybe five photos on the screen and like Sky said, they were tame. But I couldn't fucking breathe.

I felt hot all over and kind of icy on the inside. I wanted to see so much more and yeah...I wanted to do these things. I wanted to touch a guy. Not just any guy, though. I wanted Sky. Not in a rush with my eye on the clock, hoping not to get caught. I wanted time and a chance to know what he felt like without worrying that I'd kill my reputation if anyone knew. Because no one could know. My mom and Harry wouldn't care, but my team...fuck, I'd never play hockey again.

My dick deflated slightly when that last thought surfaced. Not worth it, I mused, sliding Sky's cell toward him.

"Cool. You ready to get to work?" I asked in a raspy tone.

He studied me carefully, then nodded and slipped his phone into his pocket. "Yeah."

I splayed my fingers over the keys and held my breath when he scooted his chair close. Sweat beaded on my forehead. I couldn't remember what I was doing. McGregor. Family-owned company with ten facilities. I knew the spiel. Show him the spreadsheets, explain the system. But I couldn't talk. Sky shot me a puzzled sideways glance. Before he could ask what the hell was wrong, I cupped his face and fused my mouth over his.

Fuck, he felt better than I remembered. Soft and hard at the same time. After a small grunt of surprise, Sky wrapped his fingers around the back of my neck, angled his chin, and licked my lips. I pushed my tongue between his and groaned into the connection. There was nothing pensive or uncertain here, and Sky didn't give me room to doubt myself anyway.

He nipped at my bottom lip and sucked my tongue feverishly. Our make-out session quickly escalated. I kept up and then took over, pulling him into an awkward embrace. It was the best I could do without wrestling him to the floor or on Bailey's desk before climbing over him and grinding my dick against his. I wasn't brave enough to touch him, but he had to be in the same state as me. Rock hard and slightly dizzy from it. Of course, the second I thought about it, I knew I couldn't walk away without trying.

I tugged at the front of Sky's shirt and traced the row of buttons south, pausing at his belt buckle. He hummed my name and dragged my lower lip between his teeth. I held my breath as I let my hand drift to his crotch, curling my fingers around his shaft through the khaki barrier.

"Stop."

I let go immediately and swallowed hard. "Fuck. I'm sorry. I—"

"Don't be sorry." Sky shook his head as he inched back. "This just isn't a good place. You don't want to have a coming-out moment in an office."

"I'm not coming out. I'm..." I let out a stream of air and pushed my chair away from his, swiping my hand over my jaw in frustration. "I don't know what I'm doing. But you're right. This is work and numbers and stuff and I-I'm sorry."

"Quit apologizing."

"What am I supposed to do? That's the second time I've kissed you in less than a week and the hundredth time I've wanted to do it all fucking summer. And I don't even like you. I don't know what's going on with me."

"Colby, it's pretty simple. If you want to kiss a guy and you *are* a guy, you're gay or bi or maybe you're curious. And if that's how you do curious, I'm cool with it. In fact, I want to do it again," Sky said with a lopsided grin.

I turned to stare at the computer, so I didn't do anything rash like grab his shirt and stick my tongue down his throat again. "Me too."

"Must mean you like me a little," he teased.

I gave him a weak smile. "Not necessarily. It's a physical thing. It's hard to sit next to you. Maybe it's gay or bi...all I know is, I've never had this reaction to a person before. It's like an allergy. Instead of breaking into hives, I want..."

"What do you want?" Sky prodded gently.

"You," I whispered.

"I want you too."

He set his hand on my thigh. The gesture didn't feel like a sexual overture. It was comforting and unexpectedly sweet. I hesitated for a moment; then I covered his hand.

"Now what?"

"Ask me to dinner or something."

I frowned. "Why? I don't think I could sit at a restaurant with a boner this size for an hour without passing out."

Sky threw his head back and laughed. "All right. Ask me to come over."

"Okay. Wanna come over tonight?"

"I can't. I'm busy."

"How 'bout tomorrow?"

"No, sorry. That's not good either."

I crossed my arms and glared at him. "What are you doing?"

"I'm playing hard to get. It's bad form to let a guy know you have an open calendar," Sky replied, fluttering his eyelashes.

"Cool it. No games."

Sky grinned like a madman. "Fine. Tomorrow night. Where do you live?"

I pulled out my cell and handed it to him. "Give me your number. I'll text you my address."

Sky obeyed before returning my phone. "There you go."

"Cool. Now I can give it to Miss Smartypants."

"Who's that?" he asked with a laugh.

"The cute girl from our econ class. Long brown hair, glasses, knows the answer to every equation..."

"Kendra?"

"Yeah. I ran into her at a party Saturday night. She asked for your number."

"Really? She asked me for yours a week ago."

I figured the twinkle in his eyes meant he was joking, so I rolled my eyes, flipped my phone over, then yanked his chair hard and told him to pay attention. He kicked my shin in retaliation and leaned closer so some body part was in constant contact with mine. Sky chuckled at my exasperated huff and raised an eyebrow in challenge. Sure, I wanted to wrestle him to the floor or on top of the desk and kiss that smirk off his face, but I stayed strong and somehow managed to focus on the joys of accounting.

But damn, I couldn't wait till tomorrow.

4

Patience was not my virtue. Especially when the following day was a glorified repeat of the last...pre-practice workout, practice, office, chill. The gym was easy enough. I put my earpods in and blasted some death metal music while I pumped weights. Then I headed to the rink, and everything went sideways from there.

I tuned out the conversation on the bench as I laced up my skates. It was the usual background noise that didn't require invitation to join in. Today's topics were video games, breakfast cereal, and a lighthearted discussion on masturbation. I chuckled at some stupid banter about the difference between using lube or hand lotion as I secured my helmet then slipped my gloves on.

"Dude, I never waste the good stuff on myself. It's too expensive," Ramirez said.

"You're too damn cheap. Treat yourself," Troy chided.

"Troy does...often," I teased as I grabbed my stick.

"Like you don't," he huffed lamely. "Maybe now that you have a girlfriend you won't have to."

"Fischer has a girlfriend?" someone asked.

"I don't have a girlfriend."

Troy ignored me. "She was at Schultz's party last weekend. Did you see them together? I think you broke a few hearts. Schultz told someone he thinks you'll take over as team captain and—"

I shook my head. "Nope. I'm not captain material. No way."

"Sure, you are." He turned to our teammates and raised his fist. "What d'ya guys say? Colby, Colby, Colby!"

And because timing was everything, Coach Beltram walked in.

Everyone went quiet as he cast a cool look around the cramped locker room, settling his gaze on Troy and then me.

"Good morning, gentlemen. Thank you for taking care of that line of business. Congratulations, Fischer. The job is yours." Coach barked a command for everyone to get their asses on the ice. He called my name before I made it to the exit and lowered his voice. "Hey, heads up, I have a feeling Schultz will be back. This can be a temporary gig if you hate it, or you can co-captain if you want and if he's interested. Your decision. Let's go."

He clapped a couple of times and headed for the door, leaving me frozen like a deer in headlights. Team captain? *Fuck.* I didn't want that kind of responsibility. And what did he mean by "Schultz will be back"? Sounded ominous. Like something else to add to my ever-growing list of shit to worry about.

"Hey, wait up, Fischer!" Troy hurried after me, gliding around the orange cones staggered near the entrance to the gate.

I skated backward and waved to one of the assistant coaches before motioning for Troy to talk. "What's up?"

"I'm sorry about the captain stuff, man."

"Yeah, you suck. That's the last thing I want to do."

"I didn't know Coach was there. And I'm kinda surprised he didn't leave it alone so Schultz could come back."

"Why would he come back? He's playing for the fucking Kings."

"Something went down yesterday. I think they opted not to sign him."

I skidded to a stop. "Seriously?"

"Yeah. His agent is still haggling, but he needs ice time and it looks better if he's in school, I guess, so he's coming back soon," Troy said as he made a quick loop around me. "Beware."

I squinted. "Of what?"

"You know Schultz is always looking for someone to blame. If you're team captain, you took his job, and somehow he'll spin it to make it sound like you took his shot at the big time too."

"That's ridiculous. If he wants to be captain, he can have it."

Troy tugged my practice jersey hard enough to throw me off balance. I righted myself and took a warning swing at him. He dodged me expertly and skated a few feet away, then returned and smacked my stick obnoxiously before getting in my face. See what I mean? Goalies were nuts.

"Don't be an idiot. If being captain gets you noticed, take advantage of it."

I glanced over at a group of guys doing a passing drill and gave a quick sign to let them know I was on my way over. "Coach said something about being co-captains or—"

"Only one guy wears a C on his jersey, Fischer. You know that," Troy huffed, getting in my face. "Schultz doesn't want to be your assistant and if you're his, you look like a fuckin' pansy."

He skated toward the net before I could retaliate. I would have loved to check him against the boards, but I didn't want to draw attention. And maybe he was right. If I wanted a future in this sport after college, I had to take advantage of every opportunity. Even the ones I didn't necessarily want.

By the time I left the rink and headed home to shower and change for work, I'd filed my conversation with Troy in the "things to worry about later" box in my brain. I had bigger thoughts percolating.

Like Sky.

I got dressed, brushed my teeth twice, and used extra deodorant while I talked myself into canceling tonight. Don't get me wrong, I wanted him. I just didn't know what to expect, and I didn't have a chance to talk to him privately at work. Sue pulled him in to help out on a new project, so there wasn't an opportunity to ask questions.

I gazed over the top of the cubicles and spotted him in the conference room, looking sexy as fuck in a blue gingham oxford shirt. His hair fell into his eyes when he smiled at something Sue said. I watched them for a minute or two like a creepy voyeur, and when Sue stepped out of the room, I texted him.

Are we on tonight?

Sky pulled his cell from his pocket, then looked up and caught my eye.

Yes. What time?

7? Elliot has an away game so we can hang out at my place if you want.

What can I bring? Pizza? Salad?

I squinted at my screen and marched over to the conference room. "What's with you and salad? Is that a baseball thing?"

Sky grinned and yeah...my pulse went into overdrive. "It's an everybody thing. You probably don't eat enough greens. The daily requirement is two servings of fruits and three veggies. Something tells me if I bring you salad, you'll at least get one serving."

"There was a piece of lettuce in my burger at lunch. I think I'm good. But hey, bring salad. Or just bring you." I held eye contact longer than necessary. In fact, if Sue hadn't nudged my arm on her way into the room, I might still be there. I tilted my chin and said a very dude-like “Later” before heading back to my cubicle.

THE APARTMENT WAS empty when I got home a few hours later. And clean. I stuffed the condom Elliot left on the island into my pocket and read the attached note, “Have fun. Be safe.” *Ha. Ha.*

Cool. Coast was clear. Now what? Should I turn on music, take another shower, spray on some cologne? Or maybe study a few Google entries on gay sex? No. I couldn’t do that. Sky knew I liked him…no, he knew I was attracted to him. Opening the door with a hard-on was overkill.

I jumped in the shower again, ’cause why not? Then I changed into a T-shirt and a pair of old jeans. I swiped my hand through my damp hair and paced barefoot to the living room window and back to the kitchen before grabbing a beer from the fridge. Geez, I had to fuckin’ relax. I was a head case. I popped the top open and took a healthy swig just as the doorbell rang.

Ding dong.

I set the bottle on the island and automatically hurried to open the door…with a mouthful of beer.

Sky smiled in greeting, then cocked his head.

“What’s in your mouth?” he asked, narrowing his eyes suspiciously. I didn’t answer. Obviously. I stepped aside for him to enter, willing my throat muscles to relax so I could function and you know…maybe talk to him. Sky moved into my space and sniffed before pressing a light kiss on my cheek. “Beer. Can I have one, please?”

I swallowed, blinking back tears as I motioned for him to follow me into the kitchen. I popped the cap off a bottle and handed it over with a smile.

"Did you really bring a salad?"

He held up a grocery bag and laughed. "Yeah. I was joking earlier, but I had an hour to kill after work and I figured I might have been right about the lack of vegetables in your diet. What can I say? I worry. It's nothing exciting. Just a basic romaine-spinach combo with tomatoes, brown rice, corn, and some shredded chicken."

I took the bag and pulled out a large plastic container and smaller clear one with a vinaigrette dressing. "You made this?"

"Yeah," he replied, folding the bag neatly. "Are you hungry?"

"Not right this second, but—"

"That's okay. We can have it later, or you can eat it tomorrow." Sky sipped his beer, then cast his gaze around my apartment. "Nice place. It's so...neat. Is that you or your roommate?"

I leaned against the island and let out a half laugh. "Definitely not Elliot. He's a slob."

"So, you're a clean freak, eh?"

"Well...yeah, I s'pose I am."

Sky raised his eyebrows as he perched on a barstool. "I wouldn't have guessed that. I always thought hockey players were a little rough around the edges. You are...but you aren't."

"How so?" I kicked his foot off the bottom rung of the barstool and sat down, close enough that our knees touched.

"You seem real. Real people aren't stereotypes. You're not a beer-guzzling jock who sits around scratching his nuts and watching ESPN after practice. It looks like you came home and...cleaned."

I shrugged. "After I guzzled beer and scratched my nuts."

Sky chuckled. "Naturally."

The air buzzed with a sexual current I wasn't quite ready to tackle. I needed a minute to find my balance, so I didn't spontaneously combust. *Be cool, be calm, keep it real...without being gross.* I repeated the chant in my head a couple of times before taking a drink and setting my bottle down, accidentally sliding the note Elliot left me earlier toward Sky. Who, of course, picked it up.

"No, that's—don't read that," I said in a panicky tone.

"You passed it to me."

"I did not pass it to you. You still can't keep your eyes on your own paper, can you?" I teased as I reread the note. It was rated G. *Thank God.*

Sky snorted. "Ha. Ha. What did he mean by 'be safe'? Does he think you're on a Tindr date?"

I gave him a deadpan look before pulling out the condom from my pocket. "No, but he left this."

"Ahh. I see." He chuckled lightly when I tossed it at him.

"Really? 'Cause I don't." I stood abruptly, pacing to the other side of the island. He smelled too good and was far too handsome. I couldn't think straight with him so close. Pun intended. "I don't even know what to do with that."

"You've never put a condom on your dick?" Sky asked, arching a brow.

I rolled my eyes. "Very funny."

"It wasn't really a joke. How much experience have you had?"

"Plenty. But never with a guy. We've been over this, remember?"

"Hey, I'm sorry. I wouldn't ask, but this isn't exactly a normal situation. We don't know much about each other. If it was just a matter of blowing you, then sliding a condom on before riding your dick, I wouldn't have showed up with a fucking salad."

"So, you don't bring salads to booty calls?"

He barked a quick laugh. "Never. I'm not trying to date you. I just don't know how to do this either. We have some tricky crossover now. My new boss, aka your stepdad, reminded me that he wants to have me over for dinner soon. I'm guessing that means I'll run into some embarrassing high school photos of you. It could be uncomfortable if we're not honest about what we're doing here. Or what you *want* to do here."

"You're right. So, what should we do? Eat the fuckin' salad or something?"

Sky grinned. "No. Put the salad in the fridge, then sit down and relax."

"Fine." I obeyed. I grabbed two water bottles before skirting the island and flopping gracelessly onto the stool next to him. I slid a bottle toward him in a strange sort of peace offering or a silent request to start over. Then I twisted the top on mine and took a long drink, aware of Sky's amused gaze.

"Thank you," he said, uncapping his water bottle.

I tilted my head in acknowledgment and noted a few details, like his sculpted cheekbones and the way his shirt hugged his biceps. I wished he was wearing less, but it was probably better that he wasn't. He was right. I had no clue what to do, and the work thing made it complicated. I should back off now. We could eat some salad, share office gossip, and forget about this. But...

"Did you really say you were gonna blow me and ride my dick?" I blurted.

Sky flashed a slow-growing wicked grin. The kind that instantly made my jeans feel a size too small. "I did."

"Do you like...that? I mean, being the guy who..."

"Gets fucked?" he offered. He pointed at my water bottle when I started coughing before adding, "I love it."

"Do you ever do it the other way? If we're theoretically doing this, are you gonna want to fuck me? 'Cause, I can tell you right now, I'm not ready for that."

"You know, for a badass, you're kinda dramatic," Sky said with a laugh. "I'm versatile, but I prefer to bottom."

"Bottom," I repeated.

"Top or bottom. If your dick is in my ass, you're the top. Doesn't mean you're in charge. It's just slang."

"Got it." I nodded like I knew what was going on, then shook my head...because I didn't. "Are we doing this? Or did we decide we're just talking? I can't remember."

Sky snickered. "I think we planned on doing something. But we can go slow."

"Slow as in...a hand job or a blowjob?"

"Or both."

"Okay. That sounds...good." I pursed my lips and willed my cock to behave.

"Is that what you want?"

"Yes, no. I don't know what I want. But you're here now and..."

"Do you want me to go?" he asked softly.

"No. Stay. If nothing else, we can turn on ESPN, eat salad, drink beer, and scratch our nuts."

Sky threw his head back and laughed. "Okay. So, what'd you tell Elliot that made him leave you advice and a rubber?"

"I didn't tell him anything. He has a warped sense of humor. I'm sure he thinks I'm home alone playing *Fortnite*. Do you play video games? 'Cause we can play something if you want or—"

"Maybe later. Let's just talk."

"Okay. What do you want to talk about?"

"Hockey. What position do you play?" Sky asked, peeling the label off his water bottle.

"Right wing. Forward. Think of soccer where the front line moves the ball down the field. We do the same with the puck."

"I know how it works. I've watched a lot of hockey."

"Really? Have you ever played?"

"No. Baseball was always number one for me. Besides, hockey is kind of...rough. There's always a fight. And the game moves so fast, it's hard to see the puck sometimes."

"Not if you pay attention." I raised my water bottle in a mock toast and grinned. "And I like it rough."

Sky pursed his lips and stared at me...or maybe he was staring at my throat. I couldn't tell. "Me too. But not on the field. It distracts from the game."

"In hockey, it's part of the game. If you can't defend yourself, your teammates, and the ice, you have no right to be out there. Might as well take up ice dancing or something," I snarked, only half kidding. "And no offense, but ice dancing is a hell of a lot more entertaining than baseball. Trust me, I know. I played Little League for a couple of years. I used to beg the coach not to put me in the outfield. Geez, you could take a fuckin' nap out there some days, you know?"

Sky laughed. "Fuck you. You obviously don't know what you're talking about. Baseball is a game of strategy."

"Strategy my ass," I huffed, smiling to take the sting from my words...even though I kinda meant it. "It's one of those weird sports where everyone gets pumped when nothing happens. Oh, it's a no-hitter. That's amazing. Sure...but nothing fuckin' happened! No one hit the ball, no one rounded the bases, no one slid to home plate. No one had to even wash their damn uniforms! And you know why?"

"Why?"

" 'Cause nothin' fuckin' happened," I replied, taking a long sip of my beer as I let the sweet sound of Sky's laughter wash over me.

God, he had a great laugh and a good sense of humor. It made me like him a little more.

"That just proves baseball players are smarter than hockey players," he taunted.

"Said no one anywhere ever." I held my hands up in surrender when he flipped me off. "Hey, I'm kidding. I like baseball fine. I told you I follow the Tigers. I still have the jersey my dad bought me when I was ten. Dude, I'd wear it if I still fit in it. What's your position?"

"Shortstop. I've played almost every position at one time or another, but I like it the best. You gotta be quick, have a strong arm, and good instincts. I also have a long wingspan. That helps."

"Makes sense. I don't know about wingspan, but you gotta be lightning-fast in hockey too with quick reflexes. Big ol' quads help." I smacked my thighs and chuckled. "Mine are kinda huge."

Sky gave me a lopsided smile. "I noticed. It's hot."

"You think muscular legs are hot?"

"I do. Believe it or not, it wasn't your sweet personality that made me look twice. It was your thighs."

I snickered. "That's weird."

"Maybe, but it's true. You always wore shorts to summer school. I used to come in a little late, so I'd get a good look at you before I sat down. I purposely didn't sit next to you 'cause I didn't want to get caught staring. And the one day I did, you were the one who got caught."

"Are you telling me that all this started because of my thighs?" I asked, narrowing my gaze suspiciously.

Sky nodded. "Basically...yes."

We held eye contact for a moment, then busted up.

And when our laughter faded, the mood changed all over again. I felt that same crackle of heat and sexual energy I always did when I was around him, but this time I knew what it was. And though I might have been unsure, I wasn't afraid.

I leaned forward on my barstool and motioned for Sky to close the distance. He brushed his nose against mine. I held my breath and waited for him to make a move. Any move at all. When he blinked, I licked the corner of his mouth and pressed my lips to his. We went still for a few moments; then I traced the seam of his lips and pushed my tongue inside.

One of us whimpered, and yeah, it might have been me. Just kissing him turned me on. And the scratch of his stubbled jaw was an instant reminder that Sky was all man. There was nothing soft about him. He twisted his tongue around mine, nipped at my jaw, and licked my neck before covering my mouth again, urging me to meet him thrust for thrust. It was a funny exchange of power. He took it away, then gave it back. Again and again. And every time the balance shifted, the fever grew a little hotter. Everywhere. Like the room was too warm, and we had too many layers between us. I couldn't catch my breath, but I didn't want to let go.

Sky cupped my neck and raked his fingers through my hair as he angled his head to deepen the connection. I put my hand on his shoulder for purchase and slipped my fingers under his sleeve, massaging his thick biceps. He was toned and muscular and damn, I had to see more. I crashed my mouth over his and gripped his collar to pull him closer as I unbuttoned his shirt.

He hummed in approval, reaching over to tug my T-shirt from my jeans. I broke the kiss to give him room to pull the fabric over my head. He tossed it on the island and stood to shrug his shirt over his shoulders. I swallowed hard. Yep. Just as I thought. He was fucking beautiful.

"Wow. You're..." I raised my hand tentatively and set it over his right pec. "Can I touch you?"

"Yes." Sky brushed his thumb over my jaw as he moved to stand between my open thighs.

I splayed my fingers over his chest, feeling the toned and contoured muscles. I rubbed his nipples, glancing up when he let out a low groan. I did it again and tweaked the sensitive nubs, rolling them between my thumb and forefinger.

"You like that?" I asked.

Totally rhetorical question. My spot on the barstool put his chest directly in my line of vision and a quick glance south at the bulge in his khakis told me he was in the same condition as I was. I widened my knees and hooked my fingers in his belt loop, dragging him closer so I could suck his tits, lick his six-pack, and let my hands roam freely…down his torso and along his sides before resting on his ass.

"Fuck, yes. C'mere. I want to touch you too."

Sky pulled me to my feet and wrapped his arms around me. I hissed at the feel of his warm skin, then recaptured his mouth in a passionate kiss. We made out, exploring each other with roving hands and soft sighs. I could have happily stayed like that all night long, swaying to a sweet rhythm. But maybe not. I couldn't ignore my pulsating dick for much longer. It was practically begging for release. Or at least a little friction.

We were obviously on the same wavelength. I tilted my hips and squeezed Sky's ass, grinding my pole against his as I sucked his tongue and showered his face and neck with kisses. We parted for air after a few minutes, panting breathlessly. I waited for him to make a call. He was the experienced one here. I'd do anything and everything he wanted tonight. All he had to do was say the word.

"I don't want to rush you, Colb, but—"

"Are you fuckin' kidding me?" I palmed my denim-clad erection and pumped my hips lewdly. "Please rush me. I'm dying here."

Sky chuckled as he wrapped one arm around my waist and covered my crotch with his free hand. He licked a path from my throat to my ear and whispered, "Grab your condom and invite me to your room."

I tossed the condom to Sky, smiling when he caught it midair. Then I linked my fingers with his and led the way down the narrow hallway to my bedroom. I let go of his hand and waited for him to enter. I closed the door behind him and locked it too…just in case.

We hesitated for a beat, as though a change in location might require new rules. Or maybe Sky was waiting to see if I'd freak out. But he must have seen something in my eyes, because he pounced on me. We continued where we left off in the kitchen but with a little more urgency. We were a tangle of tongues and arms. His hands were in my hair and along my back. Mine were on his ass. I rocked my hips against his a few times before stepping aside to thread the leather strap through my belt buckle.

"I gotta at least lose the jeans. They're cutting off my circulation," I said, unbuttoning, then unzipping the denim.

I pushed the jeans down my legs and kicked them off. I left my black boxer briefs on, but they left nothing to the imagination. Seriously. My dick stuck out obscenely and yeah…there was a big ol' wet spot, like I was leaking precum. Sky didn't seem to mind. He licked his lips hungrily and curled his fingers around my cock through the cotton barrier.

"You have no idea how fucking sexy this is. I don't know what I want to do first. Suck you or fuck myself on you."

"Are we gonna do that? I want to, but I've never…you know…" I bit the inside of my cheek to shut myself up. Bragging about my lack of experience with my hopeful cock pulsating in his hand was super unsexy.

"Fucked a guy?"

I gulped, then nodded. "Uh, yeah."

He smiled sweetly. "I like that about you."

"You like that I'm a dweeb who can't keep his mouth shut?"

"I like that you're honest."

"Painfully so. And speaking of painful, my dick is killing me."

"I can help you with that," he said, tightening his grip on my shaft. "But if I do anything you don't like, tell me. I'll stop."

"Okay." I slipped my thumbs under the elastic of my briefs, sighing in relief when my aching cock sprung free. I hissed a second later when he grabbed me again.

He held me at the base and leaned in to lick my lips as he stroked my shaft languidly. "Mmm. You're thick. Does that feel okay?"

"Oh, my God. Yes," I grunted.

Sky rubbed his thumb over my wide mushroom head, spreading precum as he stroked...up and down. Nice and slow. I held his gaze...and my breath, studying the flecks of gold in his blue eyes, his long lashes, and his full mouth. He looked as mesmerized as I felt. I expected cocky and vaguely condescending. Not dazed, hungry, and strung out. Knowing we were in the same state gave me a boost of confidence.

I palmed his hard-on through his khakis and tugged at his belt. "You too. Let me see you."

He kissed me as he undressed, making quick work of his belt and zipper before toeing off his shoes. When he broke the connection to shimmy his khakis and briefs over his ass, I stepped aside to give him room to maneuver. I shoved the navy-striped duvet to the edge of the bed, then lay down, propping myself on one elbow to watch the show as I reached for my cock.

Not gonna lie, I was a man on the edge. My mouth was dry, and my heart pounded against my chest. The anticipation was killing me. Sure, I'd seen my share of naked dudes in showers and dressing rooms, but no one I'd ever been attracted to. Not like this. 'Cause I swear, I almost fainted when he straightened as he stepped out of his pants. The man was a god.

No fuckin' joke. Sky looked like a cross between an athlete and a *GQ* model in clothes. With nothing on at all...he was otherworldly. Toned, muscular, sun-kissed skin, golden hair, and damn, he was hung. I licked my lips and stroked myself as he approached the bed. He flashed a lazy smile before climbing over me and settling beside me. Thankfully, he didn't give me a chance to ask any stupid questions like "What now?" He put his hand on my bare hip and scooted close, groaning aloud when our cocks collided and rubbed against each other. Sky shivered at the contact, then crashed his mouth over mine.

And we were at it again. Sucking, licking, and grinding...only it was better this time because we were naked and horizontal. I'd been in this exact situation with a few girls in the past, but I didn't remember it ever feeling quite like this. I couldn't get enough of him. I pushed him onto his back, licking his neck and jaw, sucking his bottom lip as I roved my hands down his sides and up again to capture his wrists above his head. And all the while, I couldn't control my hips. I gyrated and humped against him, loving the sweet friction. I broke for air when he parted his legs and pulled me between his open thighs.

"Don't stop," he purred.

I rose above him and tried not to shake. "I don't want to come like this. I don't want it to be over. You feel so fucking amazing."

Sky snaked his right hand between our sweat-slicked bodies and gripped us together firmly. My breath hitched in response.

"I can make it better," he said, pushing me sideways and rolling on top of me.

Maybe I should have been a little concerned about how effortlessly he moved me, but I liked it. Sky kneeled between my legs and pumped my cock a few times. I didn't care what he did next, but I kinda hoped he'd blow me. I wasn't sure how to ask or if asking was okay or—

"Oh, fuck," I growled.

He gripped my shaft and flattened his tongue before licking me from base to tip. He tapped the head against his lower lip and lapped up the precum as he held my gaze. It was literally the sexiest fucking thing I'd ever seen. But it was about to get better.

Sky teased my cock, twirling his tongue lazily over the tip, licking a path to my balls. He sucked one and released it, then did the same to the other. My nostrils flared, sweat beaded my forehead, and my heart skipped every other beat. I wanted to grab a fistful of his hair and push him where I wanted him. He sat back on his heels before I had a chance.

"Want me to suck you?"

I nodded. "Is that a trick question?"

He smiled. "No. I just want to make sure I'm not doing anything you don't like."

"I like it. A lot," I assured him in a raspy voice.

"Good."

Sky flashed a lopsided smile as he stroked my cock. He bent to lick the trail of hair leading from my belly button, pausing to trace my V-line on both sides of my hips. He hovered above me for a moment, then swallowed me whole.

"Fuck!" I cried.

Confession time. I didn't have a ton of BJ experience. A couple of girlfriends did it once or twice, but it wasn't really something they seemed to enjoy. That definitely wasn't the case here.

Sky was the pro he'd claimed to be. He hummed as he sucked, pulling back to flick his tongue around the sensitive spot under my slit before licking me like a popsicle in summertime. Then he started all over again, sucking, licking, humming, rolling my balls, massaging my thighs, and...fuck, I knew I wasn't gonna last. I pushed at his forehead and made a funny noise that didn't sound quite human. But he got the message.

"You okay?" he asked.

I pursed my lips and nodded, tearing my gaze from the erotic haze in his eyes to the sexy sway of his hips. I'd been so caught up in what he was doing to me that I didn't notice his grip on his dick. He stroked himself as he waited for my reply.

"Yeah, but I'm too close," I replied.

I groaned when he let go to climb over me. He chuckled softly as he straddled my thighs, then tapped his dick against mine like a grown-up version of a sword fight. I smiled and played along, but I kept my focus on his intense expression. He looked like the type of guy who had a million things going through his head at once. I was pretty consumed with how fucking amazing he felt, but I couldn't help wondering what he was thinking too. He looked so damn intense and—

"Touch me."

"Huh?"

Sky tweaked my left nipple. "Wrap your hand around me."

"Your dick?"

He huffed in amusement as he ran a finger along my throat, resting it on my lower lip. "Yeah, my dick. I dare you."

Very clever. I'd stroked him through his khakis, and I'd been humping and grinding against him naked for a while, but I hadn't touched his bare cock...and he noticed. I bit Sky's finger playfully and held his gaze as I reached between us to grip his thick shaft.

Damn, that was hot. He felt like me but different. Smooth skin, thick, long, veiny. The tip of his cock was wider, I mused as I dipped lower to fondle his balls. He obviously spent time manscaping. His nuts were smooth, and his sac was tight like he was ready to shoot. At least that was how it was for me when I was close. So, I tightened my hold and stroked him. Sky trembled and let out a low groan of approval.

"Is that good?"

"Yeah. Now do it to both of us."

I licked my palm, then lined my cock against his, curled my fingers around our hard cocks, and pumped my fist. "Like this?"

"Harder," Sky moaned.

"Okay, but I'm gonna come."

"Do it. Come."

I flattened my feet on the mattress and two strokes later...*boom!* That was the end of me. Cum shot over my fist and onto my stomach as waves of intense pleasure pulled me under. And a moment later, Sky was with me. I stroked him through his orgasm with a kind of wonder, as if I couldn't believe this was real and that I'd made this incredibly sexy, handsome dude come. And not just a little. My chest was covered in jizz. His and mine.

As I came down from my cloud and returned to earth, I expected to be grossed out and maybe even freaked out. I wasn't. At all. I wasn't sure how I felt, but it was something like content or even happy.

Sky dropped his head on my shoulder before flopping to lie on the pillow beside me. He pushed his hand through his hair and sighed heavily.

"Fuck, that was hot." He waited a few beats, then rolled to his side and propped himself on his elbow. "Are you okay?"

"Yeah, that was good," I replied lamely.

"Good?"

"Really good," I corrected. "Amazing. As soon as I get my breath back, I want to do it again. With lube this time."

Sky barked a quick laugh. "Okay. Just give me a couple of minutes."

I sat up gingerly and pointed at my closet. "I'll give you five bucks if you get me a towel. Top shelf on the left side. Can't miss 'em."

"Deal."

I kept my eyes glued to Sky's ass as he moved across the

room and slid the closet door open. It was a pretty perfect ass... round and muscular. My cock twitched in agreement. I caught the towel Sky tossed at me and snickered at his wide-eyed comical expression. Geez, he even looked good with a sweaty chest and a fading hard-on.

I swiped at the cum on my stomach. "Grab another towel for yourself."

Sky shook his head as he sat on the edge of the mattress and cleaned himself with the end of the towel I was using. "No need. Why do you keep towels in your closet? That's weird."

"Elliot's a great guy, but he's a towel thief and a pig. If I left mine in the bathroom like a normal person, he'd use them, leave them on the floor in his room, and I'd have to kill him. The best way to stay out of jail is to remove temptation."

"Makes sense." Sky chuckled. "Oh, you missed a spot."

He bent to lick my chin, then pushed his tongue in my mouth. I sighed into the connection, cupping his neck and angling my head to deepen the kiss as I wrestled him onto the bed and pinned him to the mattress. I bucked my hips a couple of times to make him laugh before lying on my side to face him.

"So, that was a hand job, eh?"

"Mmhmm. The deluxe version," he replied with a wink.

"I see. Kinda like getting the taco supreme at Taco Bell. Damn, I'm gonna order that every time."

Sky grinned. "Solid choice. When's Elliot coming home?"

"Tomorrow. We have the place to ourselves." I returned his smile and narrowed my gaze. "To eat salad and stuff."

"Okay. Are you hungry?"

"Yeah, a little. But...can I ask you some sex questions?"

"Sure."

"They might be a little embarrassing," I warned.

"I can handle it."

I sorted through the mental laundry list of things I wanted to know about him and me and other guys like us. There was only so much I could learn from googling. I traced a lazy circle around his nipple, then took a deep breath.

"How old were you the first time?" I held up my hand. "Oh, wait...this room is a cone of silence. Nothing goes beyond these four walls. Anything we tell each other can never be repeated. Deal?"

Sky glanced at my outstretched pinky finger. "Pinky promise?"

"Only a real schmuck breaks a pinky promise." I kept my tone light, but I was dead serious.

He curled his finger around mine and fixed me with another intense look. "Agreed. And just so you know, I'm extremely superstitious, and I tend to take things seriously. Sometimes too seriously. If you tell me something in confidence, I'll never tell a soul. I'm not saying that because I like what we just did, and I want to do it again. It's just...you can trust me."

I nodded. "Okay. So...your first time?"

"I was fifteen. Hand job with the pitcher on my team. No kissing. His rule, not mine. He was a little older than me, and he dated a lot of girls on the side. Technically, I suppose he was a dirty hookup. Whatever. Strictly hand jobs. First BJ and anal was with a linebacker on my high school football team. Randy was my first secret boyfriend."

"His name had to be Randy," I huffed sarcastically.

Sky chuckled. "Yeah. He was the kind of guy who wanted to cuddle after sex, run his fingers through my hair and tell me he loved me...that sort of thing. But then he'd ignore me at school. Not a 'Hi' or even a nod of acknowledgment. Nothing."

"Sounds like an ass."

"He wasn't. He was scared. I get it. In fact, I'm used to it. Relationships on the DL are my specialty. It's what you want, isn't it? Or is this a one-time deal?"

I frowned. "I don't want this to be it. I want to know everything. I don't know if that's a relationship thing, though. I'm just curious. But I'd never ignore you. That's not my style."

"Bullshit. You avoided me for weeks in class this summer," he huffed with a laugh.

"That's 'cause I had a crush on you, and I didn't like it."

"Ah! So you admit it!"

"Yeah, yeah. But I didn't know you. Now I do. And how would I ignore you at the office? It would be more suspicious than pretending we're friends."

Sky inclined his head. "Exactly. That's how Max and I were. Everyone on the team thought we just clicked...as friends. Now they're probably wondering what'll happen next year. Max came out and has a boyfri—"

"What? Wait a second." I furrowed my brow as I sat up on my elbow. "Your ex came out for another guy, but he wouldn't come out for you? That fuckin' sucks."

"I want to agree with you...and trust me, I was pretty unfucking-happy about it at first. But that's not how it works. Two rules in life...you can't make someone love you, and you can't tell them when to come out. The first one is just reality, and the other is personal. I was pissed at Max for a lot of reasons. I want to say I'm sad or mad he didn't love me, but the truth is, I didn't love him either. I guess I didn't like coming in second place. I still don't. We ignored each other for the last half of our season, and I haven't seen him all summer. I don't know how it's gonna go down in January. But it'll suck for the team if we don't work it out and move on," he sighed.

"Let it go. What do you care anyway? You've got me now."

Sky burst into laughter. "One blowjob and you're sold on gay sex."

"Well, yeah. And that's what we're talkin' about here...sex. Not relationships."

"Have you ever been in a serious relationship?"

"No. I usually have three-to-four-month runs with a girlfriend before I fuck up somehow or we get bored. I like the sex part, but truthfully, I'd rather be on the ice than planning movie dates. And I've been told it shows." I waggled my brows playfully. "Hey, did I mention sex? I still have questions."

He grinned. "Shoot."

"I get the basic mechanics of a hand job and a blowjob, but I don't understand anal. Part A goes into part B, but how does it fit? Not to brag or anything, but my dick is pretty big. I don't think it would work. I googled like you suggested, and the guy on the receiving end looked happy. I just don't see how."

"He's happy 'cause it feels good."

"But how? And is it clean?"

Sky snickered. "You're funny. The best sex is dirty, Colby."

"Okay, yeah, but—"

"I'm very clean," he intercepted, sidling closer as he pushed his leg between my knees.

I set my hand on his hip. "I believe you. But...hypothetically speaking, if you wanted me to put my dick in your ass, how would I do it?"

His smile spread like wildfire across his face. "You have to stretch the muscle first and get your partner to relax. Then you move carefully so you don't tear anything."

"Doesn't that kill the mood?"

"No. It's part of the mood. And you can pick up the pace right away. I like it hard and fast...in case you're offering," he added with a mischievous smirk.

"Um, yeah. Maybe...no, definitely, I want to, but I don't know if I'm ready to do it all tonight."

"There's no rush," he assured me.

"Okay. Is there an order? Like should I blow you before I try to—"

Sky set his hand over my mouth and shook his head. "No, don't overthink it. It's sex. It's fun. The best way to make sure we're both enjoying it is to talk about what you like and what you don't like."

"Like this?"

"Yeah. This may be the most I've ever talked to a potential booty call before we went all the way," he said with a laugh, "but I 'spose it's a good idea to be clear about what we want."

"Sex...and maybe salad too. I'm hungry. I think I have a frozen pizza I can pop in the oven for us." I sat up quickly, then moved to my dresser and pulled out a pair of clean boxer briefs. "Hey, one more thing..."

"What is it?"

"I need to be painfully honest here." I snapped the elastic on my briefs and continued. "I like what we did. It was possibly the sexiest thing I've ever done, and I definitely want more, but... school, hockey season, and real life are about to start again next week, and if either of us is done here at any time...no hard feelings, all right?"

"All right."

"I don't do drama well and I can't come out and..."

Sky hopped out of bed and came to stand in front of me with his head cocked. "I promise you, I learned my lesson with Max. I won't ask you to come out of the closet, and I'll try to keep my crazy under control."

"What's your crazy like?" I asked, narrowing my eyes comically as I pulled open another drawer and grabbed a pair of shorts.

"It ranges from spooky quiet to batshit bonkers. You?"

"Just your garden-variety batshit bonkers," I sighed.

Sky chuckled as he offered his hand. "This should be fun, then."

"Yeah."

I wrapped my fingers around his and squeezed. Hard.

"Ow."

"It'll be more fun if we eat. C'mon, I'm fucking starving. Let's find food," I called as I headed toward the kitchen. "Clothing optional."

We ate salad, drank beer, and talked while we waited for the frozen pizza to cook. By unspoken agreement, we steered clear of "sex" topics and stuck to "get to know you" ones ranging from music festivals to movies we'd seen recently. When a friendly debate about which version of The Joker was best got heated, I stuck my tongue down his throat to prove I was right. Next thing I knew, I was backed up against the island with my shorts and boxer briefs around my ankles while Sky sucked me dry.

We showered together, then lay on my bed, watching old Batman movies on my PC with our feet entwined. I could have suggested watching it on the big flat-screen TV in the living room, but I wanted an excuse to be close to him. I liked the way he felt against me and the way my soap and shampoo smelled on his skin and in his hair. I liked the hum of his voice and the sound of his laughter. He was intoxicating. And I was drunk on him. Maybe it was the newness of the experience. Hell, maybe I'd be over it in the morning. Somehow, I doubted that. I had a feeling that whatever we'd started had just begun.

5

Two weeks later, I didn't want this phase to end. Which was crazy, because it wasn't convenient at all. I had more demands on my time than ever. Between classes, hockey practices, and work, I was swamped. My original "last day" at the office was weeks ago. Sure, I told Harry I could come in to help out once in a while after hockey season began, but I wanted the extra excuse to see Sky. I was hooked.

It was all pretty innocent. We'd close the door and make out in Bailey's office or feel each other up in the copy room. Although he blew me in the men's restroom, which wasn't so innocent. It was hot as fuck. Just the memory of Sky on his knees bobbing on my dick made me hard. The risk and reward quotient was exciting. The thing was, I liked Sky a little more every day.

I sensed that he was extra cautious with me sometimes, like he was sensitive not to ask for too much. The funny thing was that I wanted so much more than I could say. I loved how simple conversations with him always seemed to evolve into make-out sessions with varying degrees of heat. One minute we could be debating whether milk chocolate was better than dark—and yes, I assured him it was—the next thing I knew, I was against the wall, and he was all over me. Fingers in my hair, raking my back, then grabbing my ass.

It was easier than I thought it would be to find time to be together outside of the office. Our work associates knew we were friends, so they didn't think twice about us coming in together or leaving at the same time. I'd gone out of my way to learn Elliot's new class schedule. Between his two o'clock gender studies class and his late afternoon practice, we had at least an hour to fool around before Sky had to get back to the office or I had to get to the rink. We didn't waste a minute.

We would rush to my room, lock the door, and undress as fast as possible. We dove for my bed and came together with feverish kisses and roving hands. I loved kissing him, touching him, and just holding him. We stuck to blowjobs, hand jobs, and naked grinding sessions. But every once in a while, he'd push my finger toward his hole like a gentle reminder that there was so much more we could be doing. And yeah, I wanted that too.

Sometimes, I felt as though we gave each other something we didn't get in our regular lives. Like we could drop our guards and not have to be so damn...tough. I could let him tease me without feeling like I needed to defend myself, and he could lean on me and let me put my arm around him and just...be.

Sky was easy company and seemed happy to go with the flow. For example, I had an hour between my criminal justice class and a team dinner. We had a quiz in class, so I couldn't bail early, and I couldn't be late for dinner. I suggested meeting for a drink, but Sky had a better idea.

"How'd you know about this place?" I asked, pushing open the door to the comic shop.

"I stumbled onto it last week before work. Have you been here?"

"Are you kidding me? I'm their best worst customer," I joked.

I nodded at the teenager behind the counter, then led Sky to my favorite rack of classic DC comics along the back wall.

"What does that mean?"

"I come in all the time and never buy anything. Oh wow. Look at this." I picked up a Batman graphic novel and skimmed through the first few pages.

I took a seat on a tiny stool, gesturing to the one next to me. Sky scooted the stool close and leaned against my side. We turned the pages, quietly perusing the comics for a while. The doorbell chimed once or twice, and a couple of college students meandered the narrow rows, passing us by without a second glance. We probably looked like friends who shared a passion for comics instead of two horny guys who'd settled for a Batman fix when a blow job wasn't in the cards. Then again, maybe we were both...friends and more.

I glanced sideways when I felt his stare and smiled. I opened my mouth to say fuck knows what, but Sky beat me to it.

"Do you like graphic novels or comics better?"

"What kind of a question is that? Comics, of course."

"Why don't you ever buy any?"

"I like borrowing them for a half hour at a time more. When I was a kid, my dad used to take me to a comic store by our house before hockey practice once a week. He called it comic library time. He'd buy gum or a candy bar from the owner but never the comics. Dad didn't say why, but I don't think we could afford them. He made a game out of it. We could only use the change in our pockets to buy our treat. It was usually less than a dollar and rarely anything exciting, but I love the memory. Sometimes I can smell his aftershave or tobacco in the air and... it makes me feel like he's with me," I said in a low voice tinged with a sadness I knew from experience could pull me under if I wasn't careful.

"That's cool."

"Yeah, I think so too. I'd rather have the gum now anyway. Scratch that...I want a candy bar." I made a funny face as I searched my empty pockets for change in a lame attempt to keep the mood light.

Sky nodded, jumped to his feet, and headed for the register. He returned with a single Reese's Peanut Butter cup and presented it to me like a rare and precious gift. "Ta-da. I'm gifting you my favorite treat."

I grinned. "Thanks. It's mine too. Now the real questions is... how do we share a Reese's?"

"It's for you. You don't have to share it."

"No, no. That's the rule. You have to share." I opened the package and peeled the wrapper from the chocolate. "How about if we take turns eating the outer ridge, then take a bite out of the middle?"

"So, you want to pass it between us like a joint?" he asked with a laugh.

"Yeah. Do you ever get high?" I bit into the chocolate and handed it over.

"No. I'm a control freak. I hate feeling spacey on purpose. Weed has anti-relaxing effects on me. I can't even eat it without getting antsy. A friend of mine made magic brownies once. We didn't feel anything, so we kept eating until we'd consumed the whole fucking plate. Twenty minutes later, I felt like I was swimming in a pool of flowers. It was weird as fuck."

I threw my head back and laughed. "Dude. Stay away from the brownies."

"I haven't eaten one since," he assured me, passing the Reese's over. "What about you?"

"Brownies are life."

Sky snorted. "I meant weed."

"No. Same reason, no good stories. Just not my thing."

"Mmm." He licked chocolate from his fingers and smiled. "Besides hockey and comics, what is your thing?"

"Uh...I don't know. I tend to get super obsessed about things for short periods, like video games or Netflix binges."

"I do that too. What's your current obsession?"

"You," I replied unthinking.

We stared at each other like a couple of goofballs for a few seconds before I turned the page and warned myself to pull it together.

This was getting dangerous.

IT OCCURRED to me that if I wasn't careful, I'd give myself away by fuckin' smiling all the time. It was one thing when we were alone, but walking around with a silly grin at practice or in the office was highly suspicious.

But I couldn't seem to help it.

Everyone was asking what was up with me, and they all assumed it was something different. Elliot thought I met a girl, but he didn't know who. My teammates were sure Kendra was my girlfriend and thought I was enjoying my uncontested run as captain until Schultz made an appearance too, and my mom...she was probably just happy to see me smile. According to her, I was in the middle of a decade-long Blue Period a la Picasso, and it was nice to see me enter a rosy phase. And no, I didn't come up with that on my own. Mom taught art history at the local junior college. She had a habit of comparing life to periods in art. If I had a dollar for every time she told me I had a postmodern abstract aura, I'd be rich.

I adjusted my right earpod and hummed to let her know I was still on the line while I typed. She usually texted me 'cause she I knew I didn't like talking on the phone. So, when I saw her name pop up on my cell, I answered right away. But after five minutes, I still wasn't sure what she wanted. Maybe she was curious about why I was still at the office when I'd always made a point of celebrating my last day of work in August. Now, it was September and yeah, I was still here.

"...the first week is always exciting to me, but less so to my students. Two weeks in, it can already be stressful. You seem to be coping well, though." Her statement sounded vaguely like a question.

"I'm good, Mom."

"Excellent. Do you have a game this weekend?" she asked.

"Uh, yeah. Saturday. It's more of a glorified scrimmage, though. Don't worry about missing it. Harry said you're going to Ojai."

"We are, but I was hoping I could get you to come by for dinner this week. Like...maybe Thursday?"

Ahh. Finally. "What's up?"

"You know the young man Harry hired to take over for you?"

"Who? Sky?"

I glanced over my shoulder at the partition behind me, then stood and stealthily scanned the office for Sky. I spotted him talking to Jake the snake from HR. Jake's primary mode of communication involved flirting. The guy couldn't ask for directions without giving a smarmy compliment. I tamped down the surge of jealousy and quirked my brow when Sky looked my way. Maybe the lopsided smile and the smoky glint in his eye wasn't supposed to turn me on, but my body and my brain hadn't been cooperating for months. I returned to my desk and stared unseeing at the numbers on my laptop.

"Yes. Harry invited him for dinner Thursday night," Mom said.

"He mentioned it."

"I told Harry to extend the invite to Sky's significant other, but I think he's coming solo. I'm asking you myself because you always say no to Harry, but I think it might be nice for Sky to have someone his age at the table. Are you free?"

"Maybe." I paused, then added, "I don't always say no to Harry."

"Yes, you do. You live to give him a hard time. In this case, do it for me. I think this kid has had it rough. You know how that feels and—"

"What's for dinner?" I intercepted like a pro.

"Whatever you want," she replied.

I heard the smile in her voice and felt my shoulders relax. I didn't want to rehash old family issues. Not now, anyway. They had a way of coming up on their own. No sense stirring shit up.

"Spaghetti, please."

"You got it. Love you, Colb."

"Love you too."

I disconnected the call and went to find Sky. He was at the temporary desk he'd been assigned two cubicles away from me. I knocked on the metal edge of the partition to announce myself, then sat on the corner of his desk.

Sky flashed a sweet grin as he swiveled to face me. "Hi."

"Hi. Why didn't you tell me you're having dinner with Harry?"

"Dude, you've gotta work on your wording. I'm not going on a date with him. And you already knew he invited me for dinner. Is that a problem?"

"Yeah, the problem is that now I have to go too. So, thanks for that," I huffed.

"Hmm. You don't like eating with the parents?"

"First of all, Harry isn't my parent. And second…no. I don't. But if you're there to take the heat off me, it might not be so bad."

"The heat?"

"Yeah. Cross-examination with my mom is brutal. She thinks she's subtle, but she's not. You'll see," I warned him. "I'm leaving in a few minutes for practice, and I'm not coming in the rest of this week."

"So, this is it."

"Yeah. I was supposed to be done a month ago, but then you came along and..."

Sky's smile morphed into a shit-eating grin. "You're gonna miss me, huh?"

I shrugged with faux nonchalance. "Nah."

"We can still do stuff together, you know."

I narrowed my gaze and peered over the partition to make sure no one was watching when I pumped my hips. "What kind of stuff?"

Sky snickered. "Yeah. And hang out."

"Hmm. Okay." I checked my watch, then hooked my thumb toward the corridor leading to the Barnes and Bailey's offices. "Wanna hang out now? I've got ten, maybe fifteen minutes before I need to get to practice. We could—"

"There you are! I wanted to be sure to say good-bye to you. We're going to miss you, Colby."

"Thanks, Harry, but—"

"No, buts about it! We're *all* going to miss you, aren't we, gang?"

Oh, my God. No.

I cast a quick glance at Sky, who pursed his lips like he was holding back laughter when the entire fucking office gathered around his cubicle and sang "For He's a Jolly Good Fellow" with Harry in lead vocals, singing at the top of his lungs.

Meg popped over Harry's shoulder and grinned. "Your turn, baby boy. Ice cream cake in the kitchen. I'm saving you the corner piece."

"Thanks, Meg."

There was a general whoop of glee as the entire office made a mad dash for the kitchen. I shook Harry's outstretched hand, then let out a defeated rush of air as I turned to Sky.

He set his hand on my lower back and kept it there for a long moment, the way a lover might. There was nothing sexual in the overture, but somehow that little bit of contact felt like foreplay.

"So...cake?" Sky teased, clandestinely lowering his hand to my ass.

"Fuck cake."

"Have you ever?"

"Have I ever what?"

"Fucked cake. I've seen videos of guys fucking a watermelon or a pumpkin, but not cake," Sky said conversationally.

"It's too squishy to fuck. Not to mention disgusting."

"You don't like cake?"

"I love cake."

Sky crossed his arms over his chest and grinned. "What's your favorite kind?"

"Chocolate, of course. Yours?"

He crinkled his nose and made a funny face. "I don't really like cake."

I gaped at him until he busted up laughing. "That's...disturbing. Are you gonna tell me you hate puppies and pickles too?"

Sky threw his head back and guffawed. "Puppies and pickles?"

The crew in the kitchen must have heard him, because Sue called our names and yelled something about selling my corner slice for big bucks if I didn't get my ass in gear.

I smiled, but I felt funny inside. Warm and fuzzy, but slightly nauseous at the same time. "We should go. I'm gonna be pissed if Jake the snake gets my cake."

"Oh, my God, you need to stop rhyming," he snickered.

"Fine. I gotta go. I'm gonna tell them my office replacement is a non-cake eating weirdo. Trust me, they'll love that. More for them. I'll see you at dinner."

Sky's eyes twinkled as he inclined his head. "Okay. Oh hey, my roommate is away this weekend...if you're up for a sleepover."

We shared a look and grinned.

I nodded like a puppet. "I'd definitely be up for that."

"Cool. Want me to pick you up?"

"Sure." I cast a cautious look around me before leaning in to kiss his cheek impulsively. My face felt hot to the touch when I stepped back, but Sky's incredulous expression made it worthwhile. "I don't know why I did that, so don't ask. I'll see you Thursday."

I was met with a new round of song in the kitchen. I raised my arms in the air like a rock star taking his final bow. My small loyal audience chuckled at my antics and handed me a slab of mint chip ice cream cake. I filled them in on my classes and my game schedule in between mouthfuls while stealing sideways glances at Sky.

I didn't get it. Every time he walked into a room, I lost my train of thought and got a bad case of the dopes. You know what I'm talking about...the tongue-tied, sappy feeling I knew had to be a sign of severe infatuation. I couldn't remember ever having it this bad for a girl. But Sky was doing something to me. If I were smart, I'd put some distance between us and ask a girl out. Maybe, I would. After Thursday.

THE SECOND I arrived at the rink that afternoon, I knew something was up. The locker room was a little too quiet. My teammates greeted me with cautious nods and mumbled "heys," but Logan and Troy were the only ones who looked me in the eye. I dropped my workout bag on a bench and opened my locker door noisily.

"Geez, what the hell happened? Did one of your pet turtles die, Mason?"

Mason was one of our defensive linemen. He was my height, but he had a thicker build and a nasty scar over his left brow. He looked mean as hell...and he definitely was on the ice. But he had a soft spot for animals and kept a menagerie of strange pets. Turtles, iguanas, parrots, a hedgehog.

"Not funny, Fischer," he grunted.

I widened my eyes comically as I unbuttoned my oxford shirt and was about to tell him I was kidding when I caught Logan's signal to look left.

Oh. Great.

I shrugged my shirt off my shoulders and stuffed it into my bag before turning to the small posse gathered around Schultz. I knew what was coming. And because I was one of those weird dudes who got off on confrontation, I almost hoped he'd say something stupid, so I'd have an excuse to take a swing at him. However, I wasn't a complete moron. As team captain, I was the leader here. I had to act like one. Even if it hurt.

"Hey, Schultz. Did you come to play or visit?" I called across the room.

He stood slowly and made his way toward me. He elbowed Mason aside, then crossed his arms and leaned against the locker next to mine. I hated that he was taller than me. And better looking. Oh yeah, and a better player. But if Schultz had it all, he wouldn't be here.

Schultz flashed a tight smile. "I'm playing. For now. The contract had too many holes in it. My agent thinks I can lock in something more lucrative."

I nodded. "Welcome back."

Okay, wow. Not a bad performance. I was more mature than I thought.

"Thanks."

I pulled my shoulder pads from my bag and cast an expectant glance his way. "Anything else?"

"Yeah." He shifted a little closer and fixed me with a look I couldn't quite read. It was kind of menacing, which was an interesting tactic to take with someone like me. I wasn't easily intimidated. "I want my spot back. It'll be temporary. But I need it."

I ran my fingers over the ridge of hard plastic and eyed him warily. "Need is a strong word."

"For recruitment purposes only."

"I see. So, not because you give a shit about the team," I said sarcastically.

"Of course, I do. I'm here, aren't I?"

"Yeah, and that's cool, but I'm not stepping down. Coach mentioned something about co-capt—"

"No, that wouldn't work." He lowered his voice as he moved into my space. "I need my spot back."

We engaged in an odd staring contest for a few seconds. I had to give him credit, the guy had brass balls. But I wasn't budging.

"Sorry, Schultz. I'm not stepping down. Thanks for asking." I fastened the Velcro on my pads and shot a lifeless smile at him. "If you're staying, get dressed. You're supposed to be out there warming up. We've got work to do."

"I thought we could discuss this like adults, but if I have to go to Coach, I will," he said, frowning so hard, his face contorted into a scary-looking mask.

"Go right ahead. And while you're at it, floss your teeth. You've got a piece of spinach stuck right there." I gestured at his mouth, unsurprised when he smacked my hand away.

"Fuck you, Fischer. Don't fuckin' mess with me," he snarled. "I promise you'll be sorry."

The old me would have checked him against the edge of the metal locker and clocked him in the jaw. But this amazingly new mature me just smiled. Call me crazy, but I think that was worse. He looked like he wanted to hurt me.

"Suddenly, all I want to do is mess with you. But you know what? I'm willing to forget you're an asshole...for now. The game is all that matters, Schultz. If you're here to play, you better play hard."

He gritted his teeth and slammed an open locker door on his way back to his corner. The obnoxious clang echoed in the space, startling the few stragglers who were still getting ready. Whatever tentative conversations had started while we were talking went quiet all over again.

And as I finished changing from street clothes into my practice uniform, I realized he didn't have to do much to fuck up the team's chemistry. Showing up with a crappy attitude and talking shit about me would be divisive enough to cause serious problems. Schultz could singlehandedly suck the fun out of the game for everyone.

Nah. I wouldn't let that happen. If he was a jerk on the ice, I'd deal with it. The hardest part would be to not lose my cool and end up looking like the bigger ass.

A COUPLE OF DAYS LATER, it was clear that Schultz's reappearance was going to affect the team's chemistry. It wasn't anything obvious—there were no major fights and no disruptions in the locker room, but something was off. I shared my thoughts with Elliot while I brushed my teeth and did my best not to check myself out too thoroughly. Elliot noticed weird things. He'd get suspicious if I used cologne.

I rinsed my hands, turned off the faucet, and reached for a towel. "I don't know if he really has an agent at this point, but I'd love for him to work a freaking miracle and get Schultz outta my hair."

Elliot inclined his head. "I wouldn't worry about him. He just needs to ease back into things. So, where are you going tonight? Got a hot date?"

"Uh, no. I'm going to Mom and Harry's for dinner."

"Oh. Then why are you dressed up?"

"I'm wearing Levi's and a T-shirt," I said flippantly as I checked my reflection. My hair needed a trim, but otherwise... not bad. My black tee hugged my biceps, and this was my best pair of jeans. My mom and Harry wouldn't care, but Sky always looked pretty put together...in a good way. I figured I might as well try too.

"Yeah, and they're clean," he snarked.

"Ha. Ha." I flipped the switch in the bathroom and grabbed my cell from my pocket and my keys from the island.

Elliot followed me into the kitchen. "Say hi to Mom and Harry. I'll see you tonight."

I glanced at my phone when it buzzed in my hand, then typed a quick message to Sky to let him know I was on my way downstairs before refocusing on Elliot.

"Actually, I probably won't be home tonight. I'll see you tomorrow."

Elliot leaned against the doorjamb and grinned. "Who is she?"

"What? No one. I just, um..."

"Not ready to talk about it, eh?" He held up his hands and backed away. "It's cool. But I promise I'll be nice, and I won't tell her any embarrassing stories."

"We all know you're the one with the embarrassing stories, so I think I'm safe," I bluffed.

"Oh, right. 'Member the time you sneeze-farted at the gym in front of your mom's friend who—"

"All right. I'm outta here. See ya."

I raced downstairs and headed for the parking lot on the opposite end of the complex near the community swimming pool. I pushed aside the pang of guilt. That might have been a missed coming-out moment. I could have told Elliot and even asked Sky to come upstairs and meet him, but…I wasn't ready. I didn't like keeping secrets, but I didn't want to share him and risk screwing this up either. I wanted him to be mine.

Sky waved and raised the bottle of wine in his hand in greeting when he spotted me. His breezy smile was a nice contrast to his model good looks. And maybe it was my imagination, but I swore his eyes lit up when I approached his car. I wasn't used to someone being excited to see me, and I liked it.

I pushed aside my headful of doubts and reminded myself to stay in the moment.

"Is that for me?" I asked, barely curbing the impulse to move into his space and rub my crotch against his.

"Nope. It's for Harry and your mom. I didn't want to show up empty-handed."

"They wouldn't care. C'mon, I'll drive. I have too much energy to sit in the passenger seat."

I led the way to my Prius parked under a covered carport and cast a surreptitious glance around the lot before getting behind the wheel. I waited for Sky to close his door, then yanked at the collar of his shirt and pulled him toward me. I slipped my hands around his nape and crashed my mouth over his. Our tongues dueled in a frantic give and take that left us gasping for air.

"Wow. Look what you did." Sky lifted his hips suggestively and waggled his brows.

I palmed his erection through his jeans as I brushed my fingers through his hair. Sky captured my hand and gyrated and fuck, that was hot. I squeezed his cock as I sat back, adjusting myself with a sigh.

I navigated out of the parking lot and drove by campus before turning right onto 7th Street. We rode in silence for a block or two. I debated whether or not I should try to hold his hand. But I got nervous and ended up turning on the radio instead.

Sky grinned as he shifted to face me. "How do you feel about the Jonas Brothers?"

"I feel…nothing. You?"

"I feel good things," he said with a chuckle. "Who do you think is the cutest?"

"What the fuck?" I shot him an incredulous look, then hid my grin when he busted up laughing.

"Okay, who's your celebrity musical crush?"

"Musical crush," I repeated thoughtfully. "Um…I'm gonna go with Barry Manilow."

Sky threw his head back and snort laughed. "So, you're into older dudes."

"Nah. Just kidding. My mom loves him, though. Her name is Mandy and I guarantee you, if you mention Barry, she'll tell you 'Mandy' was her first forty-five and that she listened to it over and over again. And if you don't know what a forty-five is, please don't ask. You'll get a lecture about the evolution of records to eight-tracks to cassettes to digital music. It'll be interesting for ten minutes and torture an hour later. I love my mom, but she lectures for a living."

"She's a teacher, right?"

"A professor. Art history is her jam."

"That's cool."

"Yeah. She's cool. You'll like her. Just beware…any art-related topic might lead to an accidental lecture. Hell, a conversation about peanut butter can lead to a debate about smooth versus crunchy."

"All right. Don't bring up Barry, Mandy, or peanut butter. Anything else I should know?"

"No. It'll be fine," I replied, fully aware I sounded like I was trying to reassure myself.

TWENTY MINUTES LATER, I parked in front of a two-story Spanish-style house in Palos Verdes. Neatly trimmed hedges lined the long path leading toward the iron gate and the courtyard-slash-main entrance. The homes in this neighborhood weren't as large and intimidating as some of the sprawling estates a few streets away that featured unimpeded ocean views and astronomic price tags. But it was quiet and pristine and according to my mom and Harry, it was close to LA and Long Beach, yet far enough away too.

"Very nice," Sky commented, tapping at the car window. "Is there beach access?"

"No. This section was built on the cliffs. Long Beach is closest on this end, but if you lived on the other side of the city, you'd go to an LA beach. I don't think Harry or Mom spend much time soaking up the sun," I said as I opened my door.

Sky met me on the sidewalk. "For some reason, I thought you went to high school in Long Beach. I didn't know you were from Palos Verdes."

I pulled out my sunglasses and huffed. "I'm not from here at all. And I never lived in this house. It belongs to Harry and my mother. Nothing here is mine. I'm a visitor just like you. Except I didn't bring a bottle of wine. Let's do this."

I stalked to the gate and punched in a code. When the iron doors swung open, I gestured for him to go ahead of me. Sky paused to check out the enormous fountain, then flashed a wicked grin at me.

"You're funny."

"Funny? How am I funny?"

"You're so grumpy. It's kinda cute."

"I am not cute."

"You are. You get feisty about silly things. So I got the city wrong…what's the big deal? You look like you want to fight me." He waited a beat, then whispered, "Or fuck me."

I didn't know if it was the word or the delivery or the fact that he called me out on my bullshit, but something in me snapped. I forgot where we were and moved on instinct. I grabbed the front of his shirt and sealed my mouth over his. I was aware enough to know I couldn't linger, but damn, I wanted to. I wanted this crazy push and pull and the intense exchange of energy. I'd never felt anything like this before. I'd never given one hundred percent to a lover because I didn't think anyone I'd been with could handle the real me. But maybe Sky could.

I stepped aside to adjust my junk. "We can't go in yet. Thanks a lot."

Sky chuckled. "What did I say? Fuck or Long Beach?"

"Definitely 'fuck.' " I wiped my mouth with the back of my hand and glanced toward the front door. Thankfully, the windows were shaded, but my mom would be on the lookout for us. Any second now, the door would bust open and—

"There you are!" My mom sprang into the courtyard, waving her hands above her head. "I just peeked through the peeker thing and saw your car. I was beginning to wonder if you got lost."

"Ha. No, I was showing Sky the fountain. Didn't you used to have koi fish in there?" I hugged my mom and slipped my arm around her waist.

"No. Never." Mom poked at my ribs, then extended her hand

to Sky. "I'm Mandy Cohen. I've heard fantabulous things about you. I'm thrilled to finally meet you in person, Sky."

"Thanks. I appreciate it."

Sky shook her hand, and in a few sentences managed to charm the hell out of my mother. He complimented the house, the garden, and gave her a bottle of wine before profusely thanking her for the invitation to dinner. He sounded so damn sincere, it was hard to find fault, but I did give him a "What the fuck?" look 'cause geez, this was my mom, for Christ's sake. She liked everyone.

Mandy Fischer Cohen was the best person I knew. She was warm, beautiful, kind, and smart. I inherited her brown hair and eyes...and I hoped her brain. She was five ten and statuesque with high cheekbones and a bright smile. Supposedly, she'd done some modeling in her late teens and early twenties. But she gave up a tenuous job on the runway to get her master's degree. She was famous for repeating old sayings like, "Beauty is nice, brains are sexy." Mom had both, but she tended to downplay her looks. She rarely wore makeup, and she didn't care about fashion. Though her oversized white blousy shirt, yoga pants, and bare feet worked for her.

"Hey, we eating anytime soon? I'm hungry," I said, tickling her side until she squealed and danced out of my reach.

"Good. Everything is ready. I'll have Harry put the noodles in the water now. We can start with wine and some cheese and crackers and...come on in!"

She ushered us inside the house and speed walked through the formal living space, that no one ever went in, to the great room. Harry bellowed a hearty hello from the kitchen and waved like a kid on a merry-go-round.

"You're here! Wonderful! Help yourselves to wine or beer or soda pop, then gather round the island and come visit with me while your mother puts me to work," he said with a chuckle.

"Oh, Harry..."

I rolled my eyes and steered Sky toward the bar adjacent to the island. "Pick your poison and make it strong."

"They're cool. And kinda sweet," he whispered, inclining his head when my mother leaned against Harry and kissed his cheek.

"Yeah, saccharine overload," I groused. "Two hours max."

Two hours later, it didn't look like we were going anywhere soon. Mom and Harry were both chatty and after a couple of glasses of wine, they were on a roll. They talked over each other in a manic quest to get to know Sky. Mom asked about school, baseball, what he liked about working at BBC, if he'd been to the Queen Mary. You know, random Pinot-fueled Mom questions that only she seemed to get away with. Harry patted her hand adoringly and refilled her wineglass.

I swirled the burgundy liquid in my glass, noting the reflection from the rustic Spanish lantern-style pendants over the marble island. This house was a contemporary-meets-old-world masterpiece. Wrought iron fixtures juxtaposed with glass and steel and interesting artwork hung in between arched doorways. Harry built this place for Mom after they got married, but they didn't move in until I left for college. This was their place. Not mine. I wasn't being negative. It was just a fact. Sometimes, I felt like my clearance for dinner invites was a notch above Sky's. Maybe I was being a dick, but just being here reminded me of everything I didn't have anymore.

Although tonight wasn't so bad. I stuffed myself on Mom's famous spaghetti and garlic bread and sipped wine while watching Sky politely handle their rapid-fire questions. I tried to step in a few times, but he seemed more than capable. And if I were playing the part of casual workplace friend and fellow student, I couldn't act like an overly protective boyfriend or —*Whoa! Wait a sec. Scratch that. Too soon.*

Yet as I sat next to him at the kitchen table in a house that had never felt like home, I was aware of some kind of invisible thread tethering me to him that seemed to get stronger every day. I stared at Sky's handsome profile, watching his lips move and his eyes spark with humor, and damn, I wanted to touch him. I found myself in observation mode around him. He had a talent for being outwardly friendly but not giving anything away, like he was constantly on guard. I was beginning to realize that made sense. Balancing two different pieces of your life was exhausting. Sky was a confident, no-nonsense jock, but he had a slightly nerdy side and a big-ass secret. And according to Harry, he had a promising career ahead of him in accounting if baseball didn't work out. Talk about a rough compliment. I sipped my wine and tuned in to the tail end of a conversation about teaching mid-century modern art to eighteen-year-olds.

"...the architecture and furniture captivate them. Philip Johnson's Glass House is one of their favorites. We had a very enlightening discussion about the practicality of living in a peek-a-boo house," Mom said with a laugh.

"And what do you think, my dear?" Harry asked, pushing his plate aside and leaning his elbows on the table. God, they were goopy.

I cast an "I told you so" look in Sky's direction, but he was obviously fascinated by Mom and Harry. A lot of people were. When Mom and Harry first met, everyone thought it had to be money. The twenty-five-year age gap and a significant difference in bank account balances was a major tip-off. And really, the pretty, young, penniless divorcée with a kid marrying a bald, overweight, rich guy kind of told the story on its own. But it wasn't like that at all. My mom adored Harry. Seriously adored him. She lit up when he walked into a room. And when he started talking, she got a dreamy look in her eye that might have been funny if Harry hadn't been staring at her the same way. The way he was right now.

"Keeping the windows clean would be a full-time job, my love. And I love our home," she replied in a sappy tone.

Oh, my God. Time's up. Get me outta here.

I slugged back the last of my wine and pushed my chair from the table. "We should go."

"What about dessert? I made tiramisu," Mom said, gathering the plates quickly and hurrying to the island. "Sit tight. I'll make some coffee too. You boys continue the debate. What do you think, Sky? Glass house...yes or no?"

"Mom..."

"I'll get the coffee, my darling," Harry offered.

My darling, my dear, my love...ugh. I was about to stand and put an end to dessert and coffee when Sky put his hand on my knee...and kept it there.

"I like modern architecture," he said conversationally. "But I need private space...away from windows. I like being alone."

"Colby is like that too. He hates crowds. He likes small quiet places," Mom tattled as she returned to the table with tiramisu.

"Me too. I had a fort and tent stage that lasted a few years." Sky chuckled, then thanked my mother when she slid a slice of dessert toward him. "I draped bedsheets between a desk and a chair in my bedroom and slept in a sleeping bag and pretended I was outside under the stars."

"Why didn't you just take your sleeping bag outside and do it for real?" I asked.

"I wasn't allowed to. I don't remember why. Coyotes or something."

I did a double take at the quick response. I thought he said he lived on a ranch. Didn't cowboys in training sleep under the stars at night all the time? I noted the twitch at the corner of his mouth and his white knuckles on his fork. He knew I was watching him. I captured his hand when he lifted his from my knee and entwined my fingers with his. Don't ask me why. I didn't know. It was instinctive. Like I wanted to protect him from imaginary coyotes or something. The surprising part was that he didn't let go. We held hands under the table until we were ready to say our good-byes.

Speaking for myself, it was a world record. I'd never held hands with a girl for that long. The few times I did, I was ultra-aware of stuff that shouldn't matter, like whether I had sweaty palms and if it was socially acceptable to swipe my hands on my pants if she did. With Sky, it just felt...good and right.

I slowed at the end of Mom and Harry's street, then leaned across the console and pulled him toward me. The kiss was sweet and unhurried. Like we had every right to stop wherever we wanted and lock lips...just because.

Sky inched back and inclined his head toward the house. "That was nice. You may think they're too sweet, but you should know you're lucky to be around people who genuinely love each other."

"I guess that's true," I conceded.

"It is. Are you coming over?"

"Yeah, but I don't know how to get there or what to do once I get there."

"Don't worry. I've got this part."

Sky smiled and lifted my hand. He kissed it, and I swore something inside me melted. My heart skipped a beat and then raced. I felt dizzy, yet completely in control, and more certain than I had been in a while that I was exactly where I was supposed to be.

6

Sky lived in a small box-shaped, two-bedroom house in Orange. The roots of the large sycamore tree in the middle of the lawn lifted the sidewalk and part of the walkway leading to the front door. Sky reached for my elbow when I tripped on the uneven concrete. He held my arm as he opened the door. He turned on a light, kicked the door shut, pushed me against the wall in the entryway, and crashed his mouth over mine.

His hands were everywhere at once. In my hair, on my back. He tugged my shirt from my jeans and flattened his warm palms on my sides before unbuckling my belt. And all the while, his tongue worked its own magic. He nipped my jaw, bit my bottom lip, and sucked it. I gave him space to unbutton and unzip me, then pulled him close and kissed him senseless, lining my hard-on alongside his and gyrating wantonly. We sighed at the friction and upped the tempo, plucking at clothing as we made out in a frenzy.

Sky pulled my T-shirt over my head and tweaked my nipples. "Let's go to my room. Hurry."

I barely noticed my surroundings as we bounced along the

walls down a short dark hallway. Sky kicked at a door and turned on another light. His room was small with white walls and low ceilings. The queen-sized bed covered with a plain black comforter took up most of the space. There was a nightstand, a lamp, and a narrow black dresser. The room was entirely devoid of color, and there were no hints of the person who slept here. No photos, posters, or books.

"Where's all your stuff?" I asked as I unbuttoned his shirt and trailed kisses along his jaw.

He cocked his head curiously as he stepped back to shrug his shirt off. "Here. And in the closet. Did you want a tour, or do you want to fuck me?"

"Hey. Slow down." I ran my fingers over his abs, then held his chin between my forefinger and thumb until he looked at me. "Are we in a hurry?"

"No. I just...I don't want you to change your mind."

"I won't." I kissed him quickly and lowered my boxer briefs and jeans, pausing to toe off my shoes and socks. I kicked everything aside and wrapped my fingers around my dick at the base.

"You're so fucking hot. You should be naked all the time," he whispered reverently.

I chuckled. "Thanks. I'll try it if you do. Lose your jeans."

Sky obeyed. He undressed in record time and pressed his naked body against mine before sinking to his knees to swallow me whole. I sucked in my breath and raked my fingers through his hair, wondering how this got better every damn time. I was a novice for sure, but I was already hooked. These stolen moments of fervent groping and passionate kisses over the past couple of weeks had opened a whole new world. The forbidden element added another layer that sometimes freaked me the hell out. But I couldn't deny I wanted him. All of him.

I widened my stance and grabbed a fistful of Sky's hair,

tilting my hips rhythmically. He pulled back and shot a sex-hazed glance at me. “I can take it. Go harder.”

Oh, wow. My nostrils flared as I tapped the head of my cock on his bottom lip. I should have warned him that green lights were my weakness. I took a second to gather my wits so I didn't gag him. Sky didn't give me a chance. He stroked me with a firm grip and sucked like a man on a mission. He had a very talented tongue. He flicked at the tip, twirled, then flattened it against my shaft and swallowed me again.

I watched him with a kind of wonder. He didn't hold anything back. He was completely open and honest with his body. And there was something extraordinarily hot about a masculine man going down on me like my dick was his new favorite thing while he stroked himself. Naturally, it didn't take much for me to lose control. I held his head still and fucked his mouth. The rougher I was, the more he liked it. I didn't go overboard, but I met him somewhere in the middle…giving him what he wanted, yet careful not to take too much.

Of course, I got carried away. I always did. I let go of him when he gagged and put my hands in the air in surrender. “Sorry.”

Sky grinned, pausing to suck on one of my balls, then the other before jumping to his feet and pushing me onto the bed. I rolled atop him immediately, capturing his wrists and sealing my mouth over his. He wrapped his legs around my waist and hummed into the kiss when I rocked my hips over and over in a manic quest for friction. We broke the kiss, gasping for air but didn't stop moving. I licked Sky's jaw and whispered something lame about how beautiful he was. And yeah, it was true, but it seemed like a funny thing to say to a guy in the heat of the moment. Sky obviously didn't think so.

He pushed at my chest until I met his gaze. “I want you inside me.”

I gulped. I didn't think I could speak without squeaking, so I brushed my nose against his and nodded. I moved off him and propped my head on a pillow. I stroked myself and kept my eyes on his ass as Sky leaned over and pulled supplies from the top drawer of his nightstand. He set a condom on the bed beside me, then popped open the bottle of lube and poured some on his fingers. I wasn't sure if it was a private thing, so I picked up the lube when he reached back to prepare himself. If that was what he was doing. I didn't know how this worked exactly.

And when the panic bubbled inside me, I blurted, "I don't know what to do. I feel like I'm getting it wrong. Am I supposed to watch or look away or...what?"

Sky cocked his head and smiled kindly. "You can do whatever you want. If you want to put the condom on, I can ride you and do all the work, or we can switch places. But you're not going to get it wrong. I'm here with you too. We're doing this together, right?"

I nodded. "Yeah. I just...I've never wanted anyone the way I want you."

"Believe it or not, I feel that way about you too."

Sky bent to kiss me, then leaned on his side, kicking the comforter to the end of the bed before lying beside me. He spread his legs wide and pushed a single digit in his entrance. I kneeled on the mattress and fumbled with the condom, rolling the latex on my impossibly hard length as I watched the show. And trust me, it was a good one. Sky held nothing back. He made finger fucking look like the best thing ever. I added lube and stroked myself as I scooted between his legs to get a better view. Damn, he was beautiful. I kissed his inner thigh impulsively and lifted his balls. He pushed a second finger inside and moaned softly. I caressed the sensitive skin around his entrance, licking my lips hungrily.

"Can I touch you?" I whispered reverently.

Lame, but he knew what I meant. He removed his fingers and took my right hand. I didn't hesitate. I pushed my middle finger inside him, carefully studying his expression and his body for clues. His sexy groan made me think I was doing okay, so I followed his lead and added another, then the tip of a third before he stopped me.

"I'm ready. Now."

I set my sheathed cock at his puckered hole and pushed. I paused to make sure I wasn't hurting him. His blissed-out expression assured me I was doing just fine, so I continued, slowly inching my way forward until I was completely inside him. I gazed at him in wonder and smiled.

"You feel a-fucking-mazing. Does it feel okay for you?" I asked.

Sky closed his eyes briefly and bit his bottom lip. "So good. You gotta move, though. Yeah. Just like that. Oh, fuck..."

I rocked gently at first before slowly gaining momentum. I leaned over, bracing my weight on my elbows and driving my tongue between his lips as I thrust. Sky rested his heels on my ass as he lifted his hips to meet me beat for beat. I quickened my pace, kissing him deeply as I moved. We sucked and licked at each other as the fever grew. I was vaguely aware of squeaking bedsprings, soft sighs, and insistent grunts, but I was truly lost in the moment. I'd never felt so connected with another human. It went so far beyond the physical. He looked at me like I might have answers and maybe I didn't, but I wanted to assure him I'd find them.

Sky squeezed my nipples, then raked his fingernails along my sides and reached between us. He hummed as he jacked himself. I pushed his hair from his forehead and upped the tempo until I felt the first tingle of pleasure trickle along my spine. But it was too late.

"I'm gonna come, baby."

"Do it. Look at me. Let me see you," he commanded.

I tried, but a tidal wave hit me out of the fucking blue. I collapsed on top of him, wrapping myself around his body as my orgasm took me under. But I didn't stop moving and neither did Sky. He clutched at my shoulder, then the back of my neck, pressing his forehead against mine as he stroked himself to the finish line. He let out a guttural cry as cum spurted between us. I wanted to pull him close, but I didn't want to squish him, so I hovered instead, pressing kisses everywhere...on his cheeks, his eyes, his, nose, his mouth. And when his breathing steadied, I slowly disengaged and flopped beside him.

"I wished I'd always known how great it was to be gay," I blurted.

Sky snickered as he turned to face me. "Pretty great, huh?"

"Yeah. I need to get rid of the condom. Can I use your bathroom?"

"Give me a second. We can shower together. So...you liked it."

"I loved it. I want to do it again." I kissed his nose. "And again."

He smiled shyly. "We've got all night. I'll make you breakfast in the morning. What's your favorite breakfast food?"

I sensed that hint of vulnerability I'd noticed earlier, but I bit back my curiosity and rubbed my stubbled chin against his. "Pancakes, followed closely by waffles."

"Pancakes it is. And bacon."

"Sold!"

We didn't sleep much that night. We showered, then hopped into bed and talked for hours. We stuck to safe topics like movies, music, and yes...superheroes. Somehow that led to an in-depth debate about streaming web series, which led to an impromptu viewing of a *Star Wars* cartoon he loved. We lay on his bed with our feet entwined and his computer propped on a pillow between us.

I stole sideways glances and found myself watching him instead of the show. I had a reputation for acting like an overgrown kid at times. I admit I could be goofy and immature, but I knew how to pull it together and be a boring adult when necessary. Sky was the opposite. He acted cool, calm, collected, and even a little cocky too. But I had a feeling the act exhausted him more than he let on. He visibly relaxed against me, chuckling at the animated hijinks like a kid. Or like an adult who'd finally found a safe place to rest for a while.

NEITHER OF US talked much the following morning. Lack of sleep due to sex and cartoon overload took it out of a body. I think we did it three times last night and once this morning. It was like he was on a quest to introduce me to every position in less than twenty-four hours. I fucked him on his knees, over the bathroom sink, and he rode me at least twice. He was insatiable. I was too, but my dick was gonna fall off if I didn't give it a small break.

"What time do you have to be at work?" I asked, spearing a bite of the pancakes he'd made me for breakfast.

"I don't work today. I'm on my new schedule now. I have class at ten, though. How about you?"

"I have practice this afternoon. What do you want to do about your car? Do you want me to take you to school?"

Sky picked up his coffee and gave me a lopsided smile. "I can walk. The one good thing about this place is that campus is close."

"Okay, but then what? You're still gonna need your car. How long is your class?"

"An hour. Why?"

"I'll wait. I can hang out at a coffee shop till you're done. Then we can drive back to Long Beach, and you can get your car."

"You sure you don't mind?"

"I'm positive. I'll caffeinate and people-watch."

Sky squinted as though he was trying to gauge my sincerity. "If you get bored, you can take a walk or even hang out here."

"I won't get bored," I assured him. "It'll be fun."

Famous last words. I had way too much energy to sit in a coffee shop for an hour. And I'd just had a life-altering evening. The kind that made me want to take out an ad and let everyone know. I'd just had sex with the guy I'd had a crush on for months. Gay sex. And I fucking loved it. And I really liked him. Now I had to figure out how two closeted jocks who had busy schedules, didn't live in the same city, and no longer worked together could find time to see each other. I couldn't do that sipping coffee, for fuck's sake.

Chilton College was a five-minute walk from Sky's house. I walked him to school then made my way to the Starbucks on campus. I took one look at the line of students waiting for their caffeine fix and changed my mind. I walked around the quad and was about to veer toward the main street when my phone buzzed in my pocket.

Hi Colby. It's Kendra. Call me.

I stared at the text for a second and frowned. Strange. I hadn't talked to Miss Smartypants since Schultz's party. If this was any other day, I either would have texted back or reminded myself to do so later. But like I said, nothing felt normal today and I was dangerous with excess time on my hands. So, I sat on a bench under a tree near the pillared entrance of the engineering building and pressed Call.

"Hi, Colby. How are you?" a chipper voice answered.

"I'm good. What's up?" I asked.

"Quick question. I need a date for a sorority function next weekend. Can you go?"

"I think I have a game," I replied.

"I checked your schedule. You're free that night. But that's okay. You don't have to go with me. What about Jason?"

"Schultz? What about him?"

"Do you think he'd go with me? I'm too shy to ask him."

I snorted. "You? Shy?"

"Yes. I heard he's back on the team. Will you ask him for me? Or put in a good word?" she pleaded. "Or if I just showed up at the game, maybe you could...I don't know, reintroduce us. It's been a few weeks. He probably forgot he met me."

I scooted toward the shady end of the bench. It was hot as hell in the sun, and the twist in conversation made me even more uncomfortable. I wasn't sure how to tell her that every guy on my team, including Jason, still thought Kendra and I were... together. So, I blurted it out in a rush and winced at the ensuing silence. "I didn't think it was a big deal 'cause I haven't seen you since that party. I know they'll forget about it, but if you show up to a game, they'll assume you're there for me."

"Oh. Well...tell them we broke up."

"Then why would you come to one of my games?"

"Good point. But why do they think we're still together?"

"Uh..." I swiped my hand through my hair and tried to come up with a response that didn't sound totally lame. "I didn't un-tell them anything after the party, but I will. I just don't know if I can do it by the weekend. But Jason isn't all that great a catch.

He's full of himself. And you know, there are other sports out there."

"True, but there's something about a bad-boy hockey player that gets me every time," Kendra replied with a dreamy sigh. "I don't know what it is, but..."

I listened with half an ear as she went on about aggression, passion, and masculine guys who knew how to use their hands. She was over-the-top and a little goofy too, but she was likable. I couldn't brush her off without feeling like a dick. However, I wasn't about to play matchmaker.

"I gotta run, Kendra."

"Not a problem. Good luck at your game, boyfriend. And don't forget to break up with me," she said with a laugh before hanging up.

Okay. That was bizarre and potentially alarming too. Note to self...google how to break up with a fake girlfriend, I mused as I made my way across the quad to Starbucks to meet Sky.

The campus didn't seem as congested as ours was on a Friday. There were a few students sunning themselves on the grassy knoll near the fountain, but the smarter ones stayed in the shady areas. It had to be easily fifteen degrees warmer in Orange than it was by the beach. I'd borrowed a T-shirt from Sky this morning, but his shorts didn't fit me. I was thicker around the waist than he was. I lost the battle with the Velcro and put my jeans back on. Needless to say, I was sweating bullets by the time I pulled open the coffee shop door.

I spotted Sky standing off to the side, talking to a very attractive, athletic-looking Latino and a fabulous skinny guy with platinum blond hair. My head was still spinning on the weird-ass phone call from Miss Smartypants. I couldn't wait to tell Sky about it and maybe warn him that I'd sweated through his T-shirt.

"...it doesn't have to be weird, Sky. When I'm on the field, I'm there to play baseball. That's it. I don't want drama and—"

"Hey." I bumped Sky's arm in greeting and smiled at him and his friends. "Sorry to interrupt."

"It's cool," Sky said. "I was just about to get in line."

"I'll do it. What do you want, ba—" *Holy shit.* Did I almost call him "babe" in front of strangers? I tried to cover my faux pas with a cough, then went overboard and fell into full greeter mode, like I wanted to make new friends. And I assure you, I did not. "Ha. Sorry again. I'm being rude. I'm Colby."

The hot Latino offered his hand and gave me a funny look. "I'm Max and this is my boyfriend, Phoenix."

Max.

The ex.

Fuck. He was hot. Really hot. I might have been new to owning my bi side, but anyone would look twice at the guy. Even me. His boyfriend was good-looking too...in a totally different way. Max was tall, dark, and hot while Phoenix was lean and almost pretty. He had pink lips, twinkling eyes, and a mischievous air about him. And he was staring at me with a knowing smile, like he was putting everything together and wondering how this would go down.

"So nice to meet you," Phoenix gushed with a wide grin.

I shook his hand, then hooked my thumb in my belt loop like some kind of geeky urban cowboy. "Yeah, um...you too."

"Max and Sky play baseball together," Phoenix continued when an uncomfortable silence threatened.

"Oh. Cool. Are you on the team too?" I asked. Of course, I knew the answer. I just couldn't think of anything else to say.

Phoenix threw his head back and guffawed. "Now that's funny. I don't think they'd even let me be bat boy."

Max grinned. "Sure, we would, babe."

Sky's smile didn't quite reach his eyes when he stepped aside. "We're gonna order. Later."

"Right. It's all good, Sky. No weirdness," Max said before addressing me. "Good to meet you, Colby."

I moved to the end of the line and studied the menu, then glanced at Sky. "What do you want?"

"An iced coffee, double pump, and room for milk," he replied, handing me a ten-dollar bill. "And an extra cup of ice on the side."

"I'm buying. Keep the money and text me that order. I'll never fuckin' remember all that," I groused playfully. "Go get us a table."

This time Sky's smile lit his eyes, my heart did that funny flip, and everything felt okay again. Like my weird conversation with Kendra and running into a hot ex and his new man was no big deal at all.

"Do you have time? I thought you had to get back to Long Beach."

"I have time. There's a table in the corner. Grab that one. The sun is rough out here. I shoulda taken my chances on the Velcro. Maybe no one would notice I was bustin' outta my shorts. Or your shorts. And what are you laughin' at?"

"You. You get chatty when you're flustered." He chuckled. "I'm going. I'm going."

I pulled my cell from my pocket to avoid staring at his ass. I scrolled through a few emails before casting my gaze from where Sky was sitting to Max and Phoenix, who were waiting to pick up their drinks at the counter. They knew Sky was gay. They might even suspect there was something between Sky and me. But there was an unspoken code in place not to acknowledge "us" unless we did first. I wasn't sure what to think of that.

Ten minutes later, I set Sky's drink on the table and slid into the empty chair across from him. I inclined my head when he thanked me and in a very "not so cool or calm" tone asked, "So, that's the ex?"

Sky met my gaze and squinted like he was trying to read my mind. He popped the lid off his iced coffee and stirred it lazily with a straw. "You were supposed to ask how my class went."

"Oh. How was class?"

"Good. I like the professor. Should be interesting," he said, refastening the lid and poking the straw through the plastic top. "And yeah…that was Max."

"Was he bugging you? He seemed friendly enough."

"Max is very friendly."

"Hmph. What did he say? I heard something about not being dramatic. Is he afraid you're jealous of his new boyfriend?" I whisper-hissed.

Sky shushed me before casting a wary look around us. "No."

"Well, then what did he want?" When he didn't reply, I switched tactics. "Do you want me to kick his ass? 'Cause I will. It won't be easy, but—"

"Relax, Colby." Sky snort laughed. "Thank you for defending my honor. That's cute. The funny thing is, that's what Max is doing."

"What do you mean?"

"He wants to make sure I don't mess with his man. I haven't seen them all summer, but he knows I'm a loose cannon," he huffed. "Hey, I told you I have a reputation. You keep forgetting that."

I sipped my iced latte and studied him thoughtfully. "I didn't forget. But why would he think you'd mess with his boyfriend? Are you jealous? 'Cause if you're jealous, I'm gonna be jealous."

Sky chuckled. "Don't be. I wouldn't mess with Phoenix, and I'm not jealous at all. But I was."

"Oh."

"It's not that I wanted Max back. I was the one who broke

things off. And I wasn't nice about it. I was reeling from things that had nothing to do with him, and I hated that he didn't understand. That he couldn't be what I needed…or what I thought I needed. I made him miserable. Hell, I made us both miserable." He sipped his drink and sighed. "When I dropped out of school last year for a semester, I didn't plan on returning at all. But Coach wouldn't take no for an answer. He came to see me play on the junior college team I'd joined and badgered me every day. When I explained my money situation, he cut a deal with the athletic department to give me a partial scholarship to cover all last semester's tuition and half of my last year. He made it hard to refuse."

"That's good," I replied, unsure where he was going with this.

"Yeah. But I still didn't like the idea. I knew my team would want an explanation for my absence. I couldn't exactly tell them I had a nervous breakdown after my family cut me off for being gay. But I dropped from the face of the earth and then showed up again halfway through the season like I was gonna save the day. I knew they'd hate me. I'd hate me if I were them too. I thought if Max and I got back together…on the sly, sex only…it would be an easier transition. But he'd moved on. He met Phoenix and even though he was in the closet still, he was happy."

"And you didn't like it."

"No, I didn't." He crossed his arms and stared into space for a long moment. "Have you ever…hated yourself so much you just…wanted to give up?"

"Yeah. I have. Between hormones, my parents' divorce, Mom's move, Harry, and then my dad…my teenage years sucked. But I got through it, and you did too. Or you will. And if you need anyone to talk to, you got me now."

Sky smiled. "Thanks. I think I'm getting better, but Max is

right to wonder if I'm stable. I'm not a bad guy, I'm just...not good. It doesn't mean I don't want to be. It means I'm a little messy."

"Everyone's messy, Sky."

"You hate messes."

"I hate dirty carpets and crumbs on a countertop. That's not the same thing. The things we keep inside can kill us." I set my drink between us and leaned forward, bracing my elbows on my knees. "I'm as messy on the inside as you are. Maybe worse."

"Really? Did you make veiled threats to your ex, try to ingratiate yourself to his parents who used to love you, and insult his current boyfriend because you were so fucking jealous and angry that he'd moved on?"

"Uh, no."

"Well, I did. When Max came out to our team, I was so..."

"What?"

"Lost. Hurt. Angry." Sky shrugged. "At myself. I hate that I'm scared. I hate the way I cover it, and I hate the way I hide. But it's all I've ever done. Cover, hide, pretend. So, no...I'm not jealous anymore. It was something I needed to work through, and I wish Max and Phoenix the best. I do. If anything, I wish I was brave like them. The thing is...I'm already alone. My only tie to a family of any kind is my team. I can't alienate them. I have to keep hiding. I have to pretend it's okay. Even when it's not."

"It's gonna be okay," I said softly.

"Maybe. But you've been warned. Now you know why you should avoid me. You never know when I'm gonna go bonkers," he joked.

I sidled closer and leaned against his side. "My shrink says it's not a matter of going nuts. It's a control issue. I know how that feels. Not the gay part. That's new for me. But I have a lot of practice pretending everything's cool when it actually sucks.

And I know what it feels like to be angry and to lash out at the wrong people. Ask Harry someday."

Sky grinned. "You *are* kind of a hothead."

"Understatement of the century. Are you ready to go?"

I slurped the last of my drink and tossed it into the trash can before opening the door. Sky did the same, but he kept his cup of ice. He shook a few cubes loose and chomped on them noisily as he nudged my arm.

"Were you really gonna beat Max up for me?"

I nodded, dodging a pedestrian with his eyes fixed on his cell. "Yeah. It wouldn't have ended well for either of us, though. He looks pretty tough."

"He is. He's a good guy too."

"Okay, now I *am* jealous." I kept my tone light, but I was only half kidding.

"I'm over him. I was a long time ago." He stopped at the crosswalk and shook his cup again. "I have a crush on you now. And it's a pretty wicked one."

My smile hurt my face. "Likewise. You know, I was thinking we don't really have to hide. I can just introduce you as my friend. And friends do stuff together. Not the stuff I want to do to you, but our teammates don't need to know that."

Sky chuckled as he walked backward on the sidewalk. "What kinda stuff do you want to do?"

"I don't know. Hang out, play video games, watch lame *Star Wars* cartoons...you could even come to one of my games sometime."

"Invite me."

"Huh?"

"To your game."

"Which one?"

"Any of them."

"Okay. You officially have a standing invitation to come whenever you want."

"To come whenever I want." He palmed his cock through his shorts and winked. "I like this deal."

"You know that's not fair. My dick is dying to break out of my jeans, and it's hot as fuck..." I licked my lips and glanced skyward before wiping my brow. "Geez, it's gotta be a hundred degrees."

Sky looked up as he reached into his cup and grabbed a handful of ice. He pretended he was going to eat it, then leaned and dropped it down the inside of my shirt. "Here's something to cool you off."

He darted toward his front door and I was right behind him. The ensuing wrestling match was part sexy, part fierce. I managed to get one cube in his pants just as he pulled me to the floor and rolled on top of me. After that it got a little hazy. But I did know this...under the teasing bites and good-natured fight for dominance, we'd reached a common ground based on want and need, and something more elusive that felt vaguely like finding a missing puzzle piece. The one that pulled everything together.

7

October was when life always got a little manic. If I wasn't in class, I was on the ice. We played scrimmages with local leagues during the week and real games on the weekends. And in between, we practiced nonstop. I woke up, went to the gym, went to class, then played hockey, and crashed at night only to start it all over again in the morning. It was intense, but I freaking lived for this time of year. Except now I had Sky.

We texted during the day and talked every night. I invited him over the weekend after our sleepover at his place. I introduced Sky to Elliot as my "buddy from work." Elliot was friendly, but in a more reserved way. He greeted Sky with a fist bump and made an excuse to hang out with Drew...who I still hadn't met. When I mentioned it one day, he gave me a look I couldn't quite read and said something annoying like, "I'll introduce you to Drew when you introduce me to your girlfriend."

And yeah, I still hadn't done anything about Miss Smartypants. But she didn't make it easy. In her quest to get Schultz to notice her, Kendra showed up to almost all our games and even crashed a few practices. She usually came alone and brought a stack of books and her computer with her, so she could get some homework done while she hung out. It was actually kind of cute in a geeky way. In spite of her grand gesture to show up and make herself known, she never talked to anyone but me. So even though I insisted to my team that we were just friends, her presence suggested otherwise.

"Have you even said hi to him?" I asked her when she followed me to my car one night after a scrimmage.

"Well, yes." Kendra chewed on her nail and shot a flustered glance over her shoulder as a group of my teammates passed by.

I rolled my eyes at the lascivious looks Troy and Logan gave me and discreetly flipped them off. I repositioned my hockey stick and shut my trunk before turning to Kendra.

"What's the problem? Is he seeing someone?"

"I was hoping you'd know that. He's your teammate. You see him every day."

"Yeah, well, we don't exactly get along." I tossed my keys in the air and pulled out my cell. "Where's your car? You shouldn't be hanging out at the rink in the dark on your own."

"I'm with you."

"Not really. You're using me to get to another guy," I huffed without heat.

To her credit, she didn't deny it. She adjusted her glasses and dragged her teeth over her bottom lip like she was working up the courage to ask me something I might not like.

"What if we pretend to be together?"

I frowned and shook my head emphatically. "I've been telling them for weeks that we aren't together. That was our deal. You're on your own with Jason. And what good would that do anyway?"

"Maybe he'll get jealous and try to take me away from you," she suggested. "You said he doesn't like you, and I've heard him say a few disparaging things myself."

"Disparaging, eh?"

"Yes. He called you a fuckhead when you didn't pass the disc to him."

"It's called a puck, and that's probably the least offensive thing he's called me in a while. I don't care about Schultz."

"I overheard your coach say that your chemistry sucks. He thinks Jason is spending too much time worrying about you and the scouts and it's affecting his game. And he said you seem distracted too. He thinks it's a girl. Maybe he thinks it's me anyway, so let's just make out after a game or something. What do you say?"

"You're nuts. That's what I say. Look, I like you, Kendra. You're sweet, but it's a no for me. And quit eavesdropping. It's creepy. Where's your car?"

"Over there." She gestured toward a red VW two parking spaces away.

"Get going. I'll watch you get behind the wheel. Hurry it up, though. I gotta run."

She didn't go anywhere. She crossed her arms and gave me a scrutinizing once-over. "So, is it true? Do you have a girlfriend?"

Damn, she was relentless. I scratched the back of my neck and narrowed my eyes. "I'm seeing someone. And I'm not gonna fuck it up by playing any games. Sorry."

"That's all right. I'll think of another way," she sighed heavily and headed for her car, waving before she got behind the wheel.

I waited for her to drive off, then glanced around the almost empty lot. I just told a girl I was seeing a guy. *Wow.*

Okay. So, I wasn't specific. But it still felt like a big deal. And it was true. I was secretly seeing someone I really liked. Someone I thought about every second I wasn't with him. When I wasn't on the ice, I was consumed by Sky. I jumped at every chance I had to be alone with him. And not just because the sex was off the charts.

The second the door closed behind Elliot, we'd hurry to my room, get naked, and get busy. We'd lose ourselves in a passionate tangle of tongues and come together with soft sighs and a steady rhythmic beat of our own. Sometimes we went at each other hard, clawing at skin as we fucked like madmen. Other times, we were gentle...almost sweet. And it was never the same.

For instance, in the past week, he sucked me off in the bathroom at BBC when I stopped by to see if he wanted to go to the gym. That was code for "I have thirty minutes till my scrimmage starts. Wanna blow me?" A couple of nights later, he came over after practice. Elliot was gone already, and we had the place to ourselves to do whatever the hell we wanted, so I fucked him over the kitchen island. Then we showered and played video games until he said he had to head back to Orange. He spent the night occasionally, but he usually got up before the sun to beat traffic and avoid any risk of bumping into Elliot after a sexy sleepover.

It worked for us for a month or so, but by mid-October, I wished we had more time together. And run-ins with a girl who wanted me to be her beard made me feel...trapped.

SKY CHUCKLED when I told him about Kendra's idea later that night. He draped his knee over mine and passed me the gallon of ice cream we shared while a documentary about the cosmos played in the background.

"What are you gonna do?"

"Nothing. I told her I was seeing someone."

"Really?"

"Yeah. Is that okay? I didn't mention I'm with a guy who tries to bore me to tears with geek shows. I kept it vague."

Sky grinned, then leaned in to kiss me before shifting his legs off mine and reaching for the remote. "You secretly love it."

"Yeah, right. Don't even think about pressing 'Next episode.' I'm doing head bobs over here. I'd rather watch *Star Trek* reruns."

"Oh, I bet we can find one," he said enthusiastically.

"Nope. My turn." I hijacked the remote and changed the channel to a pro hockey game.

Sky didn't argue. He leaned against the sofa cushion and propped his feet next to mine on the coffee table. He looked sexy as fuck in a pair of gray sweatpants and a white snug-fitted tee. If Elliot came home, the story was that we met at the gym and came back to chill so Sky wouldn't hit traffic. We rarely had to use any of our "stories" because Elliot didn't spend a lot of time at the apartment lately. But it was wise to be prepared.

He spooned up a helping of chocolate chunk, then passed the container to me. "Who's playing?"

"The Coyotes and the Ducks."

"Who's better?"

"They're pretty even. And they're both kinda meh. But hey, the season just started, so you never know what'll happen."

"Would you play for the Coyotes if they recruited you?" he asked.

"Hell, yes. I'd go anywhere. Kinda funny 'cause when I was a kid my dream was set and solid. All I wanted was to play for the Red Wings. No other team compared. Didn't matter if they had a better record or not. I bled for my Wings. I slept in my jersey, hugged a junior team hockey stick instead of a teddy bear, and had posters of my favorite players all over my room. If you'd told my six-year-old self he'd end up in Long Beach, California, watching teams from Arizona and fucking Anaheim play because he missed the Eastern Conferences games while he was at practice, he'd have cried himself to sleep." I shrugged nonchalantly. "Life has a weird way of rearranging your plans without any input from you."

"You sound like Calvin from *Calvin and Hobbes*. And quit hogging the ice cream," he griped playfully. "How old were you when you moved to California?"

I took another bite of ice cream before passing it over. "Thirteen. My mom left my dad and moved to California to find a better job and a purpose. Rough time for a teenager to relocate. I took it hard when she divorced Dad. The weather was nicer, but she couldn't afford club hockey until she married Harry. I took that hard too. I lived in a bigger house in a better neighborhood and I had hockey again, but I missed my dad and then...he died."

"That must have been awful." He set the ice cream on the coffee table and twisted to face me.

"Yeah, it sucked," I said, fixating on the action on the screen as I mulled over those two words for a moment.

"It sucked" didn't quite cover how debilitatingly devastating it was to lose my hero. Seven years later, the wound hadn't healed. It was open and raw. Sometimes it festered and stirred up a world of demons inside me. Other days, I put my head down and barreled through life, pretending I was okay. Although lately, I felt pretty good.

"What happened?"

"He died of a drug overdose at forty-two. He was on a toxic diet of painkillers and alcohol and...I guess he had been for a while. It got worse after the divorce. He used to call me all the time. And when the conversations started to peter, and I still didn't want to hang up, he'd tell me he was with me even when he wasn't with me. I just had to look for signs. But then he was gone for real."

"I'm sorry."

"He died alone. I can't even think about that without getting sad. Or mad. When I told you I knew what you meant about freaking out because of control issues, I was serious. I have anger management issues too. You're the one who oughtta steer clear of me," I warned him.

Sky inched closer to me and ran his fingers through my hair. "Or we should stick together."

"Maybe we should." I kissed him impulsively and smiled. "Change the subject. I don't want to get sad. Name five things that make you happy."

"Let's see...baseball, ice cream, sex, camping, and...you."

I brushed my nose against his as I plucked at his T-shirt and slid my hand under the cotton fabric to tweak his nipple. "I'm number five?"

"Yeah."

"How do I get to number one?"

Sky rested his forehead on mine and breathed deeply. "It's not really a competition, you know."

"Sure it is. I want to be number one. How do I do it? I don't know how to compete with baseball when everyone but you knows hockey is a superior sport."

He groaned loudly and pushed me away. "Mmhmm."

I climbed on top of him, straddling his legs. "Hey, it's true, and you—oh! I have an idea. It's a good one, too. Listen up. I know how to get the gold. Sex is easy. We'll just keep having a lot of it. Ice cream...same deal. Camping is a tricky one, but I'll get creative."

Sky massaged my thighs. "And baseball?"

"Easy. I'm gonna demonstrate how freaking awesome hockey is. I want you to come to my game this weekend. Watch the master at work. Then, I teach you how to ice skate."

"I told you I already know how to skate."

"Yeah, but I bet you suck," I teased. "I'll teach you how to do it the right way."

Sky laughed. "I do suck. Want a demonstration?"

"Yes, please."

I snickered when he groped my package through my gym shorts. I pulled the elastic over my shaft and held myself in invitation. He curled his fingers around me and stroked. "Maybe we should go to your room."

"El isn't coming home tonight. And if he does, we'll hear him," I moaned.

Sky twisted his wrist slightly and changed the angle. I tried to take note of his technique for future reference because the guy was a master at all things dick related. He bent to lick the tip and flick his tongue along my length before sucking me in earnest. I closed my eyes and sat back to enjoy the ride just as he pulled away.

"I want you to fuck me. Or at least touch me. Finger my ass."

Gulp. He shoved his sweatpants and boxers over his hips and kneeled on the sofa to give me easier access; then he swayed his hips seductively and bent to swallow me again. I sucked my middle finger and fondled his balls for a moment, tracing his entrance. He reached back and held my wrist steady and lowered himself on the digit.

Sky slurped and sucked me like a damn vacuum. He came up for air, twirled his tongue around the mushroom head, and did it again. And again. I fingered him to the rhythm he set and quickly obeyed when he asked for another.

"Fuck, you are so damn sexy. You love having something in your ass, don't you?" I purred.

He sat up quickly and nodded. "I love having *you* in my ass. Come on. I can't wait. You need to fuck me. We don't have a condom out here."

I followed him to my room, smiling when Sky undressed and leaned over the bed, presenting himself to me like a gift. Literally. He held his cheeks open so I could see his pucker. I licked my lips hungrily as I stepped out of my shorts and boxer briefs. Then I rolled on a condom, added lube, lined my cock at his hole and *oh, my God*...this was heaven. This was where I wanted to be all the fucking time. Buried balls deep in this man's ass. He was so damn perfect, and there was no part of him that hesitated to ask for what he wanted. "Harder, faster, spank me, like that, yes..." I fell apart with a roar, clutching his hips as I pounded his ass. Sky tensed beneath me and shivered as his release hit a moment later.

We laughed at the mess we'd made, collapsed on the mattress, and held each other for a while. I had a spent condom full of jizz on my cock, and I was pretty sure I was lying on the wet spot. Both of those things should have grossed me out. But I didn't want to move. I wanted to hold on to this feeling for as long as possible. The best part was, I knew Sky felt it too.

We were a few games into our regular season, and though I wanted to report that my team rocked or that we were at least hitting our stride and were on our way to greatness, I knew it wasn't true. Hell, everyone knew it wasn't true. We were off to a lackluster start and holding steady. The Lions led three to zero, and with two minutes on the clock in the third period, it didn't look like that was about to change tonight. Especially with Schultz sitting on the bench for consecutive penalties. Cross-checking, roughing, tripping...you name it, he did it. We were averaging three penalties per period while the Lions had one. We had no hope of winning like this.

It didn't help that Troy was a human sieve tonight and that Logan spent more time bouncing off the boards than attacking the net. So much for impressing my boyfriend with my hockey expertise. And don't worry, I kept that word to myself. I was mentally trying it on for size to see if it fit. It did…for me anyway. *Boyfriend.*

I glanced up in the stands to sneak a peek at him and did a double take when I spotted him sitting next to Miss Smarty-pants. Half a second later, the ref blew his whistle, and I promptly lost the face-off. I skated after the center, snuck up behind him and batted the puck to Logan, who raced down the ice to the net. We made a valiant attempt to score, but we didn't have a real shot on goal until Schultz came back in. He rushed the net, passed the puck to me and skated to the far right corner. The angle was close to impossible, but it was all we had. I elbowed a defender out of the way, then sent the puck across the cage to Schultz, who slammed it home.

All right. That was good.

I patted Schultz's shoulder as the crowd cheered. "Good job, man."

"Thanks, Captain. Nice pass. If you trusted me a little more, we'd do that all the fucking time. Stop being careful. We're here to fucking win," he huffed.

I veered away from him so I wouldn't accidentally trip him. Schultz was a prick, but this time, he was right. My game was always better when I let my instincts lead. When I thought too much, everything went sideways.

The same thing probably applied to my personal life. I listened to Coach's motivational speech about playing with passion with half an ear and tried to figure out what Kendra was doing with Sky. Yeah, she mentioned she had a crush on him a while ago, but she'd firmly switched to Team Schultz. Hadn't she? I couldn't decide if there was any danger in her chatting with Sky. Kind of ridiculous coming from the guy who secretly wondered if the "boyfriend" conversation was the same as a "let's not use condoms" one. Or maybe it wasn't so ridiculous. He was mine. Kendra could flirt all day with Schultz or Troy or even me...but not Sky.

When Coach finished his rah-rah speech, I added my own two cents about playing with a killer instinct before gathering my gear and slinging my bag over my shoulder. I fist-bumped a few of my teammates on my way out, then went to search for Sky.

Yep. Kendra was still there.

"Good game, Colby," she gushed.

"Thanks, but we lost," I said before turning to Sky with a half smile. I took a moment to admire him. He took my breath away. And call me crazy, but I wasn't sure what the rule was for greeting the guy who raked his fingernails down my back and told me to pound his hole last night. A high five, a fist bump? I settled for a nod of acknowledgment and a quiet, "Hi."

Kendra tucked her hair behind her ear and beamed at us. "Gang's all here. It's like a summer school reunion, right? I couldn't believe it when I saw Sky in the stands. I didn't think you two were friends. I was pretty sure you hated each other in econ."

"We ended up working together and patched things up," Sky explained. "Colby mentioned he had a game tonight, so I thought I'd come by to see if he actually knew how to skate. Nice stick, by the way."

I pursed my lips to keep from laughing. "Gee, thanks."

"Colby is a really good skater," Kendra said, slipping her arm through mine.

Her adoring look was a bit much, but it sort of made sense when Schultz paused and bumped my arm. He greeted Kendra and Sky with an absent "Hey," then hooked his thumb in the opposite direction. "Can I talk to you for a second?"

I followed him a few feet away, hiking my bag higher on my shoulder before asking, "What's up?"

"I was serious out there. That goal was teamwork at its best. You gotta feed me those shots, Fischer. Every night. You get the assist, I get the score, and we both show off our skills. And once we get our cadence down, the team will start winning. I know you don't like me, but you know I'm right."

"Maybe so," I conceded.

"Hmph. Oh, hey. Quick question. Is that your girlfriend?" he asked. Something in his tone was off. I couldn't say what it was, and I didn't waste any more time hanging out with Schultz when Sky was five feet away.

"Kendra? No, we're just...friends."

"She hangs out a lot. You must be *good* friends."

"Something like that. Later, Schultz."

I headed back to Sky and Kendra, motioning toward the exit. "I'm outta here. Bye, Kendra. Thanks for coming, Sky."

His eyes twinkled merrily. "No problem. I'd love to come again sometime."

I shot an amused glance his way, then turned when Kendra grabbed my wrist. "What did Jason say? Did he ask about me?"

"Oh, my God. Wow. Yeah, he asked if you were my girlfriend."

"What'd you say?"

"I said no," I huffed.

"Did he ask for my number or did you give it to him or—"

"No." I rounded on her in the lobby and shook my head. "And for the millionth time, I'm not going to, Kendra. Sorry. And don't ask me for Sky's number either 'cause—"

"I won't."

She glanced at Sky, standing near the door. His hair fell over his eyes when looked down to type a message into his cell. Probably to me. I hoped.

"Good."

"I think he's gay anyway. And I think he has a crush on you."

She clasped her hands and sighed. "I know you're straight, but it's kind of romantic."

"Whoa. Wait up. What makes you think that?"

Kendra pushed her hair over her shoulder and buttoned her red coat. "Clue number one, he watched you, not the game. Clue number two, he got that dreamy look I get when I stare at photos of Robert Pattinson for too long. I could be wrong. It's just a hunch. Lucky you. See you later, Colb."

Okay. That was…weird.

I met Sky outside and tilted my head toward my car. We walked side by side through the parking lot. I paused to slap high fives or shout out a greeting along the way. Sky didn't seem fazed in the slightest. He studied his phone like he had an important deal in the works and didn't look up until I opened the trunk and threw my bag inside.

"You were pretty good out there tonight, Fischer."

I chuckled. "Thanks."

"I wish the pants were a little tighter, but still…I was impressed."

"Even though we lost?"

"Yep."

"Where'd you park?" I asked.

"On the other side of the rink," he replied.

"Hop in. I'll drive you. None of my teammates park over there. We can talk without drawing attention."

"Relax, Colb. Two guys sitting in a car isn't necessarily gay," he chided, fastening his seat belt.

"True. But if Kendra sees us, she might get the wrong idea." I filled him in on my brief conversation with her as I drove around the perimeter of the rink.

"Wow. I didn't realize I was that transparent." He rubbed his stubbled jaw and stared out the window.

"I'm not too worried. Are you?"

Sky shifted sideways in the passenger seat when I parked in the far end of the lot where it was quieter. "No. She doesn't know me. I won't come to any more games, though. I don't want to draw attention to you or me or—"

"No." I covered his hand and linked my fingers through his unthinking. "We're doing just fine. Kendra is cool. She's just... odd. But in a harmless way. And she likes me. She's not gonna start any rumors. Besides, I liked knowing you were there tonight. Even though it was a little distracting. I didn't play well at all. I think I was too aware of you. Kind of like I am right now."

"What do you mean?"

"My skin feels tingly. And I'm holding your hand, which means any second now, my palms are gonna get sweaty. You have no idea how much I want to kiss you right now." I shot a nervous glance his way before fixating on the halo aura around the streetlight in the parking lot. "It was sort of ironic that the girl who wants me to pretend I'm her boyfriend was sitting with the guy I wished I could have greeted properly."

"And what's proper?"

I loved the ready humor in his tone. I gave him a lascivious wink. "I would have stuck my tongue down your throat for sure."

Sky barked a quick laugh. "I'd dare you to do it now, but Kendra might be watching."

"Let's go to my place."

"I thought Elliot was home tonight."

"Oh, yeah. Fuck." I started the engine and shrugged. "I still have to shower. Follow me home. We can grab something to eat or go to a movie or something."

"Sounds good. Oh, by the way, Harry asked me to house-sit next weekend," he said as he opened the passenger side door. "I'm supposed to water plants, pick up the mail, and run a couple of errands for him."

"What? Why? Where are they going? No one fuckin' tells me anything."

"Your mom might not know. It was spur of the moment. Between the commute and roommate issues, I think Harry feels sorry for me."

"What's up with your roommate?"

"Micah's a pig. And he's got this hero-worship thing for me that bugs me. He was new to the team last year. He was supposed to take my place, but he's not all that great, so he got bumped when I came back."

"Hmm. That's like Schultz and me. Except we still don't like each other."

"Micah just likes to choose sides. Everyone knew there was tension between Max and me. And when most of the guys rallied around Max, I got stuck with Micah," he said with a self-deprecating half laugh. "He's an okay guy, but he's a crappy roommate. Harry overheard me telling Sue that he left a piece of pizza on the bathroom counter."

"Gross."

"I know. And you know Harry. I think he wants to save the day. This is his version of buying me a new bike. Or giving me a temporary reprieve from sadness."

I cocked my head. "That's a funny way to put it."

"Maybe, but I'm not too proud to take him up on it. So, what do you think? Do you want to help me water the plants?"

"Fuck, no. But I'll watch you water the plants." I waited a beat, then added, "Naked."

Sky chuckled and leaned toward me like he was going to kiss me. He caught himself at the last second "Oops. Sorry. You're kind of irresistible."

He hopped out of the car and said something about meeting me in the parking lot at my place. I nodded in acknowledgment, but my head was churning with some weird-ass thoughts. I didn't like that Harry wanted to take Sky on as a project. That was my job. Well, not my job...but I was Sky's person, and I didn't like that my mom's husband was once again jumping in to pick up the broken pieces. House-sitting wasn't a big deal, but it was strange that my mom hadn't mentioned it to me. And it was strange that Schultz was the voice of reason in tonight's game. I *had* been holding back. I'd been playing cautiously. I was known for taking chances on the ice, so what the hell was wrong with me? In my effort to do everything right, I was doing everything wrong. And don't get me started on Kendra. Her astute observations rattled me.

There was a fine line between control and instinct. If I tried to control too many variables and curb my instincts, something important might get lost. I just hoped it wouldn't be me.

If I needed any further clues that my world was upside down, my friends chimed in with a few hints Monday morning. Troy and Logan gave me shit for not showing up to a party after the game on Saturday. They told me Schultz was making a move on my girl, and I'd better watch out. I knew Kendra was the one chasing Schultz, but my blank stare must have looked slightly menacing 'cause they backed off right away. The truth was...I didn't know about the party until it was too late, because I'd ignored my cell all night.

I wouldn't have gone anyway. I was with Sky, and I wanted him to myself. We'd grabbed dinner at the pier and walked along the boardwalk. And even though neither of us would have called it one, it felt like a "date." The non-touchy kind. I didn't have a ton of dating experience, but girls seemed to like it when you tried to hold their hand or steal a kiss in public. Knowing I couldn't do those things with Sky was frustrating. However, it also made every accidental touch feel like foreplay. Seriously. He put a hand on my elbow to steer me out of the way of a fast-moving skateboarder, and my dick perked up and my heartbeat went into overdrive.

So no, I wasn't sorry I missed a stupid party. But I realized I had to pay more attention to my friends. Especially Elliot.

My mind was whirling with a to-do list after my morning workout. I had just enough time for a shower and a super quick breakfast before class. I yanked my sweatshirt over my head and moved toward the hallway, then stopped in my tracks and did a double take when I spotted Elliot lying on the sofa with a blanket over his legs. His unruly hair was messier than usual, and his eyes looked puffy.

"Dude, what's up with you? Are you sick?"

He shook his head, but he didn't look at me. "No."

"What's wrong?"

"Nothing."

Monosyllabic answers weren't Elliot's style. The guy could talk. And he wasn't one to lie around on a Monday morning without a good reason.

"You've got five seconds to spill the beans. I'm rank. I need a shower and food and I need to get to—"

"Drew broke up with me."

Oh.

That stopped me. It felt like a punch in the gut, which was weird since I'd never met the guy. I sat on the coffee table and narrowed my eyes.

"What happened?"

He stared at something over my shoulder before letting out a sad sigh. "Nothing, really. I think I'm too young for him. Too immature, too inexperienced, too loud, too silly. Take your pick. I'm just not what he's looking for."

I furrowed my brow angrily. "Then he sucks. Screw him. You can do better."

Elliot quirked his lips in a reluctant smile. "Thanks. I kinda thought you'd be happy I got dumped."

"Why would you think that?"

"C'mon Colby, you've been avoiding me like the plague for the past few months. You didn't want to meet Drew, and you're conveniently never around whenever I'm home. I get it. You're uncomfortable."

"What? No. I'm not. I'm—" I swallowed the words before they threatened to spill. *I'm bi too. I'm head over fucking heels for a guy, and I'm quietly going crazy because I can't tell anyone.* I told myself this wasn't the time for a confession and that Elliot didn't want to hear about my drama while he was dealing with his own. Of course, I was just scared. Really scared.

"It's okay. Don't beat yourself up. Give me a few days to wallow in self-pity. Then we can hit the bars and go back to normal. And you can introduce me to your girlfriend."

"Huh? Oh. Right. Yeah…" I stood abruptly, knocking his foot off the edge of the sofa to lighten the mood when a cloud of doubt and doom threatened to suffocate me. "I gotta get to class."

"Later. I'll be here all day if you're looking for me."

I headed down the hall, wiping my sweaty palms on my T-shirt. I set my hand on the knob and turned back to the living area.

"Hey, El…don't believe him. You're not too much or too little of anything. He's just not the person for you. You'll meet the right guy. Or girl."

Elliot smiled, then sat up and opened his arms. "Thanks, Colb. Wanna give me a hug?"

I rolled my eyes and flipped him off before hurrying to get

ready. I could beat myself up for being a coward, an asshole, and a rotten friend later.

I CALLED my mom after class later that afternoon. If I was a bad friend, chances were good that I was failing in the son department too. And I had a few questions for her.

"Hi, honey. How are you?"

"Fine. How come you didn't tell me Harry asked Sky to house-sit for you this weekend?" I blurted.

She didn't say anything right away. I hated the hint of silence. It reminded me of darker days when she was constantly on edge around me. Before I could find a smoother way to re-ask the question, she replied.

"Well, I called you yesterday. If you'd returned the call, it might have come up then. Is there a problem? I thought you and Sky had become good friends."

I hiked my foot on the cement bench outside the school auditorium and studied the scuff marks on my Converse. "Who told you that?"

"Harry. He said you're still going by the office regularly, and since you typically avoid Harry and the office when you don't have to be there, we both assumed you and Sky were close."

"Well, yeah. I just thought you'd mention asking him to house-sit when your son lives ten miles away and could easily handle the unnecessary chore of watering your two plants," I snarked.

"Do not take a tone with me, Colby. And don't misconstrue a friendly gesture into a 'Harry is the bad guy' scenario. He likes Sky. He feels sorry for him. His parents aren't in the picture, and other than you, he doesn't seem to have a lot of friends. And he's struggling to make ends meet. Since you're good buddies, I'm assuming you know all that," Mom said patiently.

I pulled my sunglasses from my collar and put them on before flopping onto the bench.

"Yeah, I know."

"Then let us show him kindness. I can't imagine any parent cutting off their child. It's evil and unthinkable. I hope you know I'd never do that to you. You could come out as a Sharks fan and I'd still love you," she joked.

I snickered at her lame attempt at humor. "That will never happen."

"Well, I'd love you anyway. I'm making a lasagna and freezing it for Sky. Anything else I should get for him?"

"Ice cream," I replied automatically.

"Okay. Any special flavor?"

"He likes everything. Especially chocolate chip. But if you could get five gallons that would be great."

"Five gallons? Oh, I see," she said in a "mom" voice, "I'll make sure there's plenty to share...if you happen to come by the house to keep him company. And I'm sorry we'll miss another game. I'll be at the next one for sure. Now, are you okay?"

I assured her I was fine and changed the subject as I made my way across campus. I peppered her with questions about their upcoming winery trip to deflect her attention from me... and Sky. I wished I hadn't said anything. I wished I wasn't such a dick about Harry. I chuckled to myself because Harry and dick in the same sentence would always make me laugh. Then I thought about her casual "coming out" comment and immediately sobered.

She didn't know about Sky and me. She couldn't. We were careful and very hetero-acting. We didn't give anything away. Did we?

8

"This house is insane. A stocked fridge, movie-sized flat-screen TV, a pool, a hot tub...I could get used to this."

Sky raised his beer in a toast, then took a sip and set it on the edge of the hot tub next to mine. He propped his elbows on the ledge and stared up at the starry night sky. I draped my legs over his and flattened my hand over the bubbles in the water.

"Hmm. This feels good. I lost count of how many times I got shoved against boards tonight. My muscles are so sore," I groused.

"This will help. My dad always insisted I use the hot tub after games and practices to relax my muscles. He may be an asshole, but he was right about a few things. I didn't like sitting in a hot tub when I was a kid, though. I always wanted to be in the pool."

"Hmm. Me too. I never lived in a house with a pool, though."

"Really?"

"Really. We didn't have one in Michigan. My dad took me to the public pool once in a while when it was wicked hot in the summer. And when I moved here, Mom had a condo in Long

Beach before we moved into Harry's place in Naples. It was right on the water, so the beach was my pool."

"Must have been nice," he replied idly.

"It's was fine, but I hated it. I would have hated anything, though. I told you I wasn't a fun teenager," I admitted with a wry half grin. "I really hope I don't have kids like me someday."

"Do you want to have kids?"

"Yeah. I think so. Do you?"

Sky rested his head on my shoulder. "I don't know. I'm afraid I'd fuck up. You'd be a good dad, though."

"What makes you say that?"

"You're fun, but you know when to get serious. You're smart and you're generous with your knowledge. You're kind without being a pushover. And even when you get mad, you don't blame anyone else for your mistakes."

I cocked my head curiously, then ran my fingers along his jaw. "Thanks. I'd like to think that's all true. But when I get mad, I kinda lose my shit, so I don't know."

"Oh, please. When was the last time you totally lost your shit?"

"Tonight. I got in a fight with a fucker from the other team who shoved Logan so hard, he ricocheted into another player and left an opening for his right wing to score. It was a dirty play, and if the ref wasn't going to call him on it, I was."

Sky grinned. "God, I love it when you get all badass. Wish I could have seen it in person."

"You had to water the plants," I teased, leaning in to kiss the corner of his mouth impulsively.

"True. And put the lasagna in the oven," he said, waggling his brows. "Back to your badness...hockey doesn't count 'cause it's practically your job to fight."

"Let's see..." I tapped my chin thoughtfully. "Um, I think I lost my cool when you looked at my paper in summer school, and I got accused of cheating."

Sky kissed my neck and palmed my cock under the water. "That actually turned out okay, though."

"Mmm. True. I guess I haven't totally come undone in a while. It was a daily thing in high school. If I didn't have hockey and friends like Elliot to pull me out of my room and remind me life could be good, I might not be here."

"What do you mean?"

"I was ready to check out when my dad died. Everything seemed kind of...hopeless, meaningless. Everything I worked for was never going to become what I hoped it would. And the one guy who made anything seem possible was gone. I didn't think I had much to live for," I said softly. "But I wasn't ready to die...so I just made everyone else's life miserable. Seemed fair at the time. Now I know I was just a prick. I feel bad about some of the things I did and said to Harry. Poor guy. I used to see how long I could go without talking to him. I went a whole week once. I didn't answer his questions, I didn't look at him at dinner. My therapist suggested it was a case of misplaced anger. I think I yelled at her," I deadpanned.

Sky smiled. "Mmm. Sounds reasonable."

"It wasn't. But it's hard for the average fifteen or sixteen-year-old who's grieving to come up with the right words to tell the universe it fucking sucks. So, I blamed Harry. And every time I came home with a crappy attitude, moaning about everything from school to a lack of mosquitoes in the summer and sunshine all damn year, Harry would just...smile and tell me he understood. That pissed me off more. And one day, I lost it. I mean...*lost* it.

"Everything set me off. They were serving pizza instead of chicken nuggets in the cafeteria, the girl I had a crush on told me Billy Hauser asked her to prom, my binder broke in the middle of homeroom and my notes went flying....You name it, it happened. None of it added up to much, but I wasn't home, and I didn't have anything or anyone I could rely on to make it better. I missed my friends in Michigan, I missed my old team, my old coach. And I really fuckin' missed my dad. So much...that I sat on the front porch and listened to his old voice messages."

"You saved them?" Sky asked.

"Yeah, I still have 'em."

I jumped out of the hot tub and grabbed my phone from on top of our clothes. I sat on the ledge, next to Sky, and scrolled through old voice mails until I found what I was looking for.

"Hey buddy, I was at the rink today and I ran into Gretzky. He says 'I hear your boy is gonna give me a run for my money someday.' I told him to watch out for Colby Fischer. Okay, none of that happened, but it will. Keep working hard. And don't forget to fuckin' call me. It's boring as hell out here without you. Love you, kid."

I sighed heavily and tossed my cell toward our clothes before sinking into the water again. When I spoke again, my voice was thick with emotion. "That's from nine years ago. I haven't listened to that one in a while, but after he died, I needed to hear Dad's voice every day. I used to torture myself with these. I thought it would help, but on bad days, they made everything go dark. Like the day of the broken binder...I went inside and found Harry and Mom canoodling in the kitchen. All I could think after my initial 'God, that's gross,' was that Harry stole my life. It was his fault that I was here, and my dad was dead, and my mom loved him, and I'd never get a real shot to play hockey, and blah, blah, blah. You know, teenage angst times ten."

"Sounds kind of normal."

"Sure, until I went to my room and fucking shredded it. I threw books and furniture, slashed a pillow and tore a comforter, and broke down like a kid. My mom started crying and Harry..."

My nostrils flared and my eyes blurred with tears. I blinked at them furiously and swallowed hard.

Sky caressed my arm, then gently put his around me. "What did Harry do?"

"Harry was Harry. He was kind and careful and steady. He kept saying he understood. Over and over again. 'It's okay, I understand.' That's all."

"He's a good guy."

"Yeah, but he wasn't the guy I wanted, and I hated him for it. It's taken me a long time to accept that change happens, grief happens, and life is totally unfair sometimes. Harry didn't deserve all that BS. We're in a good place now, but I feel bad when I think about the shit I used to say to him. Don't get me wrong, he still bugs me. Incessantly happy people are freaking weird. Am I right? But he's a good guy, and he makes my mom happy, so I try not to roll my eyes too loudly when he tries to save the world," I huffed in amusement.

Sky chuckled. "Do you think he's trying to save me?"

"Probably."

"Someone should tell him I'm a lost cause."

"Not me. I think you're pretty amazing," I gushed, slipping his beer bottle from his hand and tipping it back.

"That's because I suck your cock," he countered.

I knew he was kidding, but the flippant remark pissed me off. I set the bottle down and glowered at him.

"No, that's not why. If you never sucked my dick again, I'd still think you're amazing. This isn't just about sex anymore, Sky. You aren't my bi experiment. You're more than that to me."

Sky cocked his head in surprise. "Colby, I'm not..."

"You're not what?"

"I'm not good enough for you. You can do so much better than me. I'm not special. I'm the opposite of special. I'm everything you thought I was when you first met me. You shouldn't trust me or want me. I'm a liar, a thief, a sinner. My own family kicked me out, for fuck's sake. They'd been quietly pushing me away for years, but when I actually said the words out loud... everything changed."

"How'd they push you away? What do you mean?"

"I wasn't just into baseball. I liked other things...less masculine things. Every time they caught me playing with my sister's Barbie or dancing to a 'girlie' song, I had something taken away. I can't tell you how many nights I'd sit in my room, staring out the window at my family sitting around a bonfire in the backyard, roasting marshmallows and telling ghost stories. Or the camping trips I wasn't included in because I might embarrass my dad in front of his friends. I have a million stories like that. What I don't have is sweet messages to listen to from people who loved me and wanted only the best for me. I'm not one of the special ones, Colby. I'm...broken."

I punched the water and rounded on him. "Fuck that!"

"Hey, I know it sucks, but—"

"No, it doesn't just suck...it's wrong. Don't put yourself down or tell me I shouldn't trust you. Your parents are the ones who are wrong. They're the broken ones. And they're evil fucking cowards for pushing you away and making you doubt yourself. Fuck, it pisses me off."

"I can see that," he said softly.

"If someone has the guts to come out, they deserve respect for sharing something that is no one's fucking business."

"Calm down, Colby. The neighbors can hear you."

"Fuck them too." I waved dismissively, then pointed at his chest. "I want you to start over now. Really start over. Day one. Cut out that toxic bullshit. Come out to me now."

He furrowed his brow in confusion. "What do you mean?"

"Say the words. Tell me who you are."

"I'm gay," he deadpanned. "Is that what you—"

I took his face in my hands and kissed him hard. When I was sure we were both breathless, I pulled back and rubbed my nose against his.

"Good. I'm glad you're gay. I'm glad you exist. And I'm proud of you for walking away from them. It takes a lot of strength to start over. So, I don't see broken. I see someone who fell down and got up, over and over again. I see someone with big balls and a big heart. I'm glad I know you, and I'm so fucking glad you're mine."

"Yours," he repeated in a kind of daze.

"Yeah, and don't tell me you're not, 'cause you are. I don't care if no one else knows. We know."

"Wow. Where have you been all my life?" He regarded me for a long moment, then laid his head on my shoulder. "God, you feel so fucking real...and safe."

I held him close and kissed his temple. "I am safe. I'm your safe place. You can tell me anything, and you can be anything you want with me. If you want to dance around the yard naked, go for it. If you want me to buy you a Barbie, I'll do it."

Sky bit my bottom lip and snickered. "I don't want a Barbie, but thanks."

"I know how to build forts."

"You do?"

"Yeah, I'm good at it." I kissed his nose and gently pushed away to climb out of the hot tub. "I have an idea, but it's too cold to do it out here. Let's go inside."

I threw Sky a towel and dried off before picking up our clothes and running to the house. I dumped our stuff on the sofa and told him to grab some ice cream. Then I went to the linen closet in the hallway and pulled a stack of sheets and a couple of blankets down and met him in the living room.

"I got the chocolate chip and two spoo—what are you doing?"

Sky set the container and the spoons on a side table and put his hands on his hips. He was buck-ass naked and extremely drool-worthy. I took a moment to admire him as I pushed the coffee table out of the way and lay two comforters on top of the Persian rug. I unfolded a sheet in his direction and inclined my head.

"We're building a fort. It's a naked fort. No clothes allowed. Tuck that end into the back cushion on the sofa and I'll secure this side behind the chair." I snapped the sheet when he didn't move. "What are you waiting for?"

"I...I don't—this is really um...sweet."

"Yeah, well, hurry up. The ice cream is gonna fuckin' melt," I said in a faux-gruff tone.

Sky chuckled and got to work. Within ten minutes we'd erected a cavernous indoor tent. It was actually too big, so we redid it and made it a little cozier, keeping a small opening so we could see the TV and the lights from the pool outside. Then we leaned against the sofa, shared ice cream, and just...talked. And after a while, we lay down on the bed of blankets and made out.

We took our time. Sweet, sexy kisses morphed into deep passionate ones with twisting tongues and roving hands. He licked a trail from my chest to my cock and paused to play with my balls before sucking me to near oblivion. I pulled his hair to stop him, pushed him to his back, and crawled over him to return the favor.

"Colb, you don't have to—"

"I want to," I assured him, stroking him languidly. "Relax, baby. Let me take care of you."

I was new to giving blow jobs, but I was a quick study. I copied Sky's technique, licking his shaft a few times before taking as much of him in my mouth as possible. I sucked his dick eagerly, bobbing my head, and kneading his balls while he chanted my name above me. When he warned me he was close, I rolled on a condom, and slowly made my way inside my man.

We'd done some version of this dance countless times over the past few weeks. Sometimes we were rough and a little nasty. I liked that I didn't have to be careful with him, and the raw carnal element of fucking like animals with complete abandon was freeing in a way I couldn't quite explain. But this was pretty damn amazing too.

I stared into his eyes as I moved, rocking my hips over and over, whispering sweet nothings. Except I meant every word. He was beautiful, he was good, he was mine. And when the rhythm changed, I pumped a little harder and held him closer until he wrapped himself around me, dug his heels in my ass, and begged for more. We clung to each other when our release hit at the same time. And in that split second, I felt a sense of absolute rightness. Like the stars were aligned as they were meant to be. It was up to me to figure out the way from here.

BASIC RULE IN HOCKEY, and maybe in life...never take your eye off the puck. Easier said than done. A single puck could move at speeds close to a hundred miles per hour if it was hit hard enough. Life was more like practice when the ice was littered with dozens of pucks and small orange cones that were supposed to test your agility, dexterity, and speed. Everyone could see the nets on either side of the ice, but if you knew anything about hockey, you knew it was a hell of a lot harder than it looked to score. And if it seemed easy, something was probably wrong.

So yeah, in the weeks after our weekend staycation at Mom and Harry's when everything seemed to gel and click...personally and on the ice, I should have been wary as fuck. And I should have known it wouldn't last. In my defense, there were too many pucks on the ice. I couldn't fucking see all the ways everything could fall apart.

First mistake, I narrowed my field of vision to school, hockey, and Sky. I didn't go out with my friends or make an extra effort to hang out with Elliot. I didn't have time, and I figured everyone was in the same boat. Second mistake, I naïvely assumed that because the team was finally winning, everyone was happy. Third mistake, I forgot about Kendra.

That last one was completely understandable, right? We were acquaintances at best. We had one class in common last summer, and she had a crush on my teammate, and she thought my boyfriend was gay. And he was, but still...when she stopped calling me and coming to games, I honestly thought she'd moved on. Big mistake.

But Kendra was not on my radar at all. There was no room for anyone but Sky. I loved being with him. He was smart and funny, and he seemed to like my rough edges and warped sense of humor. And he was always game to get out and do something physical like hike Runyon Canyon, kayak in the bay, or just go to the park near his place in Orange and throw the baseball around. His roommate, Micah, invited himself to tag along a couple of times.

He was a little dopey, but he adored Sky...platonically speaking. If Sky gave him a tip about his balance or form, Micah stopped everything and listened. I met a couple of his other teammates at the batting cages once too. At first, I was bummed to share his time, but I was curious to see him around his guys. He'd made it seem like a rough transition back to normal after his hiatus, but that wasn't my impression. His teammates respected his skills. Sky was crazy talented. He had a rocket for an arm, and he was a great hitter. And I do mean great. Their catcher, Javi, joined us one Saturday in early November. He pitched a couple of balls to Sky and threw his hands in the air after Sky hit five in row over the fence. Micah howled with glee when Sky ran imaginary bases in the deserted park.

I picked up the bat and chuckled. "Dude, don't take it so hard. He's pretty damn good."

"He's not bad," Javi agreed.

"He's fuckin' awesome," Micah corrected. "Better than Max the mo."

Javi rounded on him menacingly. "Shut the fuck up, Micah."

I cast a wary look between them. They were both over six feet with broad shoulders and big ass muscles. I wasn't shy about jumping into a fight, but I had no idea what the hell it was about, and I had a game that night. I had to conserve my angst for the ice. Sky pushed them apart and glowered at them.

"What's going on?"

"I called Max a homo. Big fuckin' deal. It's what he is. I have no respect for that shit," Micah spat.

Sky shoved Micah hard enough that he almost fell on his ass. "You'd better fuckin' find some respect, asshole. He's one of us."

Javi and Micah both stared at him incredulously like they couldn't believe Sky would stick up for Max.

I mentioned it when we were loading his equipment into my trunk. I took a swig of water, clandestinely reading his expression for a clue when he took too long to answer. He looked angry, as though he was spoiling for fight.

"Hey, you okay?"

"Yeah, but that..." he pointed to the empty expanse of greenery beyond the parking lot. "That's just a taste of next season. Micah's an idiot, and idiots love to talk. It's not gonna be pretty."

"You know what you need?"

"Sex."

"True, but that might have to wait, so let's do the next best thing," I suggested, bumping his arm before heading for the driver's side.

"Where are we going?"

"We're going ice skating, baby."

Siri hooked us up with a rink five minutes away in Anaheim. Sky didn't say much on the short drive. He didn't complain about my idea, but I figured that was because his mind was on other things. Crappy things he couldn't control. I parked the car, then squeezed his hand.

"You know the problem with baseball players?"

Sky rolled his eyes. "No, what?"

"You have too much time to think. You sit around waiting for the action to get going, and your brain goes bonkers. If you played a real sport like hockey, you wouldn't have a chance to think, you know what I mean?"

Sky looked down at our hands and at me. "You're holding my hand."

"So what? We don't know anyone here. And I promise I won't do it in the rink."

"I wish you could," he said softly before letting go to open his door.

I stared after him for a second, then grabbed my skates from the trunk and met him on the sidewalk. I joked around about how gross rental gear was while he strapped his boots on and laced them.

"Two words...foot fungus. Make that three words...athlete's foot fungus. I hope your socks are thick. It's bowling shoes times ten 'cause you know your feet are gonna sweat."

"Why would my feet sweat?"

" 'Cause you're nervous," I replied, leading the way to the ice.

"I'm not nervous."

"Yeah, you are. You're afraid you're gonna fall and I get it, but don't worry, I'll catch you, baby."

Sky swatted my hand away with a laugh before gliding onto the ice. "You're forgetting something....I know how to skate."

I watched him weave through the weekend skaters with the ease and grace of a dancer. He moved toward a less crowded area, then pivoted to skate backward, flashing a wide, radiant grin at me that made my heart thump like a drum. I slowed to observe him with a dopey smile on my face. No one should look that good under fluorescent lights, bopping their hips to an old Katy Perry song, I mused as I picked up speed and almost took out a fellow skater.

I pulled at her elbow to steady her and apologized.

"Totally my fault. I'm so slow on these. This is what I get for trying to—oh! It's you."

Fuck.

"Kendra. Hi. What are you doing here?"

"Funny you should ask. I'm practicing. For Jason. I told him I could skate, but I'm not very good. If he sees me during free skate at the rink by us, he'll think I'm trying to impress him. And I totally am, but don't tell him. We just started seeing each other. Well, sort of...we had coffee and he kissed me. I can't tell if he really likes me or if he's playing around. What are you doing here? Oh, let me guess. Which one is she?"

"Huh?"

"Your new girlfriend. I told Jason you must be seeing someone, because you never go to any parties anymore. And you had a super goofy look on your face before you bumped into me. Gotta be a girl," she said, grasping my forearm for balance as she glanced around the ice.

"Uh, no. I'm with Sky," I blurted. "He lives out here."

"Oh." She cocked her head and squinted at me suspiciously. "Are you guys...more than friends?"

I stared at her like a deer in headlights. The direct question caught me by surprise. The answer was on my face. It didn't matter if I denied it.

But I did.

"Uh…no. Ha. I'm…we're—"

"Hey, Kendra. How's it goin'?" Sky asked, coming to a graceful stop beside us.

"Good," she said, glancing between us. When she let go of my arm, I could practically see her putting puzzle pieces together in her head, and there wasn't much I could do to stop her.

Sky bumped my shoulder as if to pull me from my trance. "You two are so quiet. What did I miss?"

Kendra shook her head, then opened her arms to balance before pasting a smile on her face. "Nothing. I'm here with my sister. Our parents live nearby and…"

She rambled on for a minute or two about fuck knows what. I tuned her out and did my best not to freak out as I weighed the possible damage she might do. She was dangerous because she didn't mean any harm. A couple of mistimed words could really fuck up my life, though. Or maybe I was being dramatic. I studied Sky, nodding his head and chatting amicably with her. For all I knew, he was the one giving us away. The longer I stared at him, my mind shifted to other thoughts. I wanted to ask when he learned to skate, who taught him, and if he knew any tricks. I wished my tongue didn't feel so damn heavy.

"…throwing the ball around at the park with a few of my teammates, but I think Colby has to get back to Long Beach soon," Sky said, nudging me again.

"Yeah, I do. Um, see you around, Kendra."

"You'll see me tonight. I'll be at the game," she replied cheerily. "But I'm done here for the day. I don't think my ankles can take much more. Later, boys!"

I watched her wobble on the ice, then glide toward the nearest wall for purchase.

"Are you okay?" Sky asked.

I scratched my stubbled jaw and pursed my lips. "Honestly... I'm not sure."

We didn't stay at the rink for long. I wasn't good company, and I couldn't articulate what was wrong in the middle of family skate time. I was quiet on the short drive to Sky's place. I pulled up to the curb behind Micah's ancient Toyota and smiled when he grumbled about having to deal with his roommate.

"He'll probably act like nothing happened. Asshole." He hooked his thumb and motioned for me to open the trunk. "I need to get my stuff. Are you coming in or—"

"She knows."

Sky went perfectly still. "What do you think she knows exactly?"

I gave him a quick rundown of our exchange and let out a ragged breath. "I wanted to tell her not to say anything, but if I had that's the same as admitting we are a couple, right? I can't win."

"Do you think she'll say anything to Schultz? She's not malicious, you know."

"No, but she's a talker. I'll pull her aside after the game. Hopefully, I'll figure out how to word this without coming out," I said, raking my fingers through my hair. "This wouldn't be a big deal if Schultz wasn't in the picture. I know this sounds paranoid, but I wonder if he's using her against me. Like he's trying to take my girl behind my back. He's the kind of dickwad who uses weird power plays."

"Hey, stop spinning on it, and keep your head in your game. I was going to come by for the second half after I meet up with some of the guys. Maybe I shouldn't, though."

"No, I think the key is to act normal. I'll mention something in passing and keep it light. Kendra is cool. This isn't a big deal."

"Okay." He squeezed my hand, then opened the passenger door. "Wish I could kiss you right now. It would be a sloppy, wet one."

I smiled. "Gee, I'm bummed I'm missing out on that."

"You should be. See you tonight. And hey...no freaking out."

9

I freaked out. It was a low-grade freak session that began the second I stepped into the locker room that night. There was a hum in the air I didn't trust. It sounded like white noise and nerves, and there was no reason to be nervous, because the Ravens sucked. Tonight's game was a glorified scrimmage. Nothing to worry about.

But something was wrong. I just couldn't put my finger on it.

Coach gave his usual pregame speech, then stepped aside to talk to Schultz while I gave a mini pep talk. It was something lame about not getting lazy even though we knew the competition wasn't fierce.

"We'll be fine as long as Troy keeps his legs closed," I joked.

Troy flipped me off and sidled closer. "Don't worry about me. Schultz has it out for you tonight."

"Huh? Why?"

"I don't know. He's acting weird. Did something happen with you and Kendra?"

I huffed in exasperation as I reached for my helmet. "Geez, no! We're not—"

"Hey, relax. I'm just the messenger. I think he's making a

move on her to piss you off and stir up shit. Don't let him get to you." He patted my back and moved to his locker to finish dressing just as Coach gestured Schultz and me over.

"What's up, Coach?"

"We've got a couple of scouts in the crowd. Do your thing and remember, you make each other look good when you work together. No bullshit out there." He nodded briskly, then headed for the exit.

I furrowed my brow and turned to Schultz. "What the hell did that mean?"

"He doesn't want me to call you a faggot on the ice," Schultz said matter-of-factly before fastening his helmet and pushing past me.

The entire team stared like they sensed a train wreck about to happen. Everyone knew the tracks were wonky, the weather was bad, and everything was moving too fast. But the momentum was building, and there was no way to stop the inevitable.

So, here's the thing about me. I didn't mind a good fight. Or even a bad one. I'd had my share of scars, bumps, and bruises from this game. Not much fazed me. If I felt backed into a corner, my natural reaction was to punch my way out. If someone was an asshole, you dealt with it then and there. It took me a while to grasp the difference between a good fight and a stupid one but, even I knew, I couldn't do much about Schultz. Not now, anyway. It was game time.

We demolished the Ravens. It wasn't much of a challenge. They were undermanned, and the guys they played were cautious to a fault. Stealing the puck from their forward was like taking candy from a baby. Schultz had two goals, and I had a hat trick by the end of the second period. Coach sat us both at the beginning of the third, and that was when things went south.

Schultz chugged a water bottle, then screwed the cap on it and gestured toward the stands.

"Your boyfriend's here, Fish."

I looked 'cause I'm an idiot like that, and yes, Sky had just arrived. He stood in the aisle and was about to take a seat when Kendra waved him over. I glanced sideways at Schultz and huffed.

"Fuck off."

"At least you didn't deny it," he taunted. "What's it like doin' it with a guy? Are you on top or is he or do you take turns and—"

"Schultz, Fischer! New line," an assistant coach called.

I grabbed my stick and stepped over Schultz, "accidentally" shoving him back on the bench when he stood. I glided onto the ice and skated toward the puck, passing it to Logan, then cutting off a defender so I had an open angle at the goal. Schultz moved in front of me and hedged me out just as the puck flew in our direction. He drove it home and let out a whoop as he sped around the ice for a victory lap with his fist in the air.

"What the fuck was that?" I growled as I skated beside him.

"That was called a goal, gay boy. I know you want to get another one for your man, but you gotta be quick out here."

"You keep it up, I'm gonna kick your ass, Schultz."

"Do it. I dare you."

To the average observer, I bet our conversation looked tame. Schultz had a shit-eating grin on his face and I was mostly calm...but not quite. There were five minutes on the clock. I could make it a couple of minutes more and not come undone. I hoped.

Nope. Ten seconds later, he was at it again. "Kendra told me, you know. She wasn't specific. I just put together that you don't have a girl. You have a guy. I'm right, aren't I?"

"Fuck off."

"Sure thing, buddy, but you never said who does who. He looks like he has a big dick. Can you get the whole thing in your—"

I checked him so hard, his head hit the plexiglass. He dropped his stick, pulled off his helmet and his gloves, and came at me, cocking his fist and punching my jaw. The flash of pain acted like a triple shot of adrenaline. I chucked off my gloves and my helmet too and started swinging. I heard gasps from the crowd, whistles screeching, and people yelling, but it didn't stand a chance against the white light. The only way out of that tunnel involved pain. I connected once or twice more until someone pulled me away. I looked down at the blood on my knuckles and my jersey, then over at Schultz's smug expression just as he mouthed, *Thank you, Captain.*

I wasn't sure what he meant until I was in a quiet locker room struggling to get dressed as quickly as possible. I couldn't deal with my guys looking at me like an alien while Coach lectured us about sportsmanship, selfish play, ugly execution. I pulled a T-shirt over my head and concentrated on putting my shoes on without wincing.

My ribs hurt and my jaw felt swollen. In the melee at the end of the game, Schultz and I had been hustled off the ice and treated for minor wounds. I'd been released first, so I hurried to the locker room, speed-showered and was mostly dressed before the team trickled in. I didn't know where Schultz went, and I didn't give a fuck. I just wanted out.

Call it cowardice if you want, but as the seconds ticked by and my internal fight or flight mechanism went bonkers, I realized I had three choices...confirm, deny, or stay silent. I was a fighter, for sure. But I wasn't in this alone. I couldn't out Sky.

I zipped my bag, picked up my stick, and slipped out the side door. I raced to my car, threw my stuff in the trunk, and took a deep breath, willing my hands to stop shaking. Typing a simple text message was hell.

I'm going home. I need to talk to you but I—

Tap, tap, tap.

I dropped my phone on my lap and jumped in my seat. Sky rapped on the window again and motioned for me to open the door. I obeyed quickly, then turned on the engine, and peeled out of my parking spot before he had a chance to fasten his seat belt or ask questions.

"What the fuck happened?"

I couldn't respond right away. It took everything I had just to concentrate on getting the hell away from the rink. And that didn't feel right on so many levels. Ice was my happy zone. It was the one place that felt like home no matter where I happened to be. Michigan, California...zipping through traffic and running red lights to make a getaway while an ancient Alice in Chains song blasted in the background seemed surreal. And wrong.

But I didn't know how to make anything right. Or if it was even possible.

I slammed on my brakes behind a truck when traffic slowed around campus. Then I wedged my hands under my thighs and glanced over at Sky.

"I'm sorry," I whispered.

"For what?"

"Everything."

"Colb, it's gonna be okay."

"No, it not. I'm..."

"You're shaking," he said, rubbing my arm and reaching for my chin. "Geez, you're gonna have a black eye. What happened?"

I jerked away, continuing down 7th Street before turning left on Bellflower, screeching around the corner and into my apartment complex. I killed the engine and pulled the key from the ignition…and froze. Fuck, I had nowhere to go. I didn't know if Elliot was home, but I couldn't waltz through the door with Sky, especially when I looked like this. He'd want to know what happened. I have to tell him, and then he'd know too and…

Oh, my God.

This was what Sky meant about coming out. This shit was real. And scary. I didn't think I could do it.

I covered my mouth to silence a scream bubbling in my throat and let the first tear trickle down my cheek unchecked.

"I don't know what to do," I choked, swiping at my face.

"Colby, you're scaring me. Tell me what—"

"They know about us."

"Who knows?"

"Kendra, Schultz. He was taunting me on the ice. He wanted me to lose my shit. And I did. I gave him everything he wanted. I proved I can score, but I crumble under pressure. No doubt he's telling the whole fucking team I'm gay, and you're my boyfriend and yeah, I should be back there…defending you and defending myself and calling him out for being a rotten fucking human, but—"

"But what?" he prodded, unbuckling his seat belt and setting his hand on mine.

I looked at him across the darkened car and damn, he crushed me. I expected him to panic along with me, tell me I'd ruined his life, and his shot at making it to the big leagues. But he seemed more worried about me than himself. He obviously didn't get the severity of the situation.

"I couldn't out you too," I replied.

"Oh. Right."

"So, we have to figure out a story. This isn't sustainable. I'm going crazy. I can't go inside. Elliot will want to know what's going on. I can't go back to the rink. I need a story. I need us to be on the same page, so I don't mess up your life or—"

"Don't worry about me. Tell me what you want to do," he intercepted calmly.

"Me? I'd like a one-way ticket to Mexico right now. That's what I want," I snarked, pushing my hand through my hair. "After that...I don't know. I didn't think I'd have to come out. I thought we could do this and keep quiet and if it got intense, we'd part ways...no harm, no foul. But coming out...I don't know if I'm ready."

"I understand," Sky whispered.

"So, let's think of something believable." I unbuckled my seat belt and twisted sideways. "I look guilty as fuck for walking out of there tonight. I'll say my mom was in the stands and she made me go to the ER to get checked and—"

"Was she there? I didn't see her."

"Thankfully, no. She's visiting my aunt in Tucson. She'll have questions too. Whatever. I'll deal with that later. We can say that we're really good friends, which is true, but maybe you need a beard. I'll say you're dating some girl at Chilton or that you—"

"No."

"Do you have a better idea? Speak up now 'cause my phone is lighting up and I need reasons for tonight. I need someone to tell me what to do. I need you to help me, Sky," I pleaded, swiping at the fresh round of tears welling in my eyes. I didn't get it. I'd never been a crier. This was a sure sign I was a man on the edge.

"Okay." Sky brushed my cheeks tenderly and licked his lips. When he spoke again, his voice cracked. "I'll let you go."

"Huh?"

"Just deny it. Just pretend we never happened. It's your word against theirs. If you don't want them to know, then don't tell them."

"Right. That's what I'm saying. So you'll do the same thing. Just pretend you don't know me. Okay. We can do that, but when will we see each other?" I asked, dragging my teeth over my bottom lip.

"We won't. We can't."

"What...wait. Are you saying we're over? Or are you saying you *want* to come out?"

"I don't want you to come out if you aren't ready, Colb. And I don't want to stand in your way."

I squinted in the dark. "I feel like you're saying something else. If I come out, you're out too. Would you be okay with that?"

Sky stared at me for a long moment, then inclined his head. "Yeah. I would be."

"Oh." I sat back. "I didn't think you would be."

"That's because you're not ready. And that's okay. Look...I tried to force it once. But I won't do it again. I'll never ask you to do something you aren't comfortable with."

"Yeah, but we can still see each other, you know."

Sky shook his head. "I don't want to pretend anymore. I can't be with you and act like you aren't the only person who matters to me. It's probably best if I just...fade away."

I opened my mouth and closed it like a fish out of water when Sky got out of the car. I hopped out quickly and raced to the other side.

"You can't leave me, and you don't even have your car. Talk to me. There's gotta be another way."

"There is no other way. We can't have it all. Maybe it's not fair, but life isn't fair. People love lies. They love to tell them, analyze them, pull them apart, and expose them. No one wants to hear the truth. It's scary and it's a little too human. And the truth is, I care too much about you to let anyone pull you apart or beat the shit out of you on the ice because of me."

"Trust me, he looks worse than I do," I huffed.

"I believe you. You're tough, baby. But you're scared too. I don't want you to be sad or scared. I don't want you to resent me or wish you'd never met me. And I'm not going to stand in the way of your dreams. I love you, Colby. I only want you to be happy."

"You love me," I repeated, licking my lips.

"Yeah." Sky stuffed his hands into his pockets and nodded. "You're the best thing that's ever happened to me. And the best thing I can do for you is let you decide what you want on your own. No fear, no guilt, no pressure."

"Whoa. Wait, wait, wait." I held my hands up and blocked his path. "What if I want this? You and me..."

Sky put his hands on my face and sealed his mouth over mine in a possessive kiss, then released me and stepped backward. "Take your time. You'll know when you're ready."

I watched him walk away and disappear into the shadows. I was bruised and scratched and sore all over. My body ached and my head pounded. But it was nothing compared to the hole in my heart. The utter desolation penetrated my bones and left me feeling...empty and more alone than I'd ever been in my life.

I trudged through the quiet complex and up the stairs to my apartment. Elliot greeted me absently from his perch on the sofa. I grunted, heading to the kitchen to grab a water bottle. Elliot called my name before I turned down the hallway.

"Hey, did you guys win?"

"Yeah."

"Cool. Come play FIFA 20 with me, dude. Tell me how awesome you were while I kick your ass," he said.

"No, thanks. I'm gonna crash. I'm tired," I said, leaning on the corner of the wall.

Elliot sat up and cocked his head. "It's eight o'clock. *Whoa.* Rough game? You look like you got run over."

I gingerly touched my sore jaw. "Schultz has a mean right hook."

"Schultz did that?" he asked, standing to inspect my wounds. "What the fuck?"

"He looks worse."

"What happened? And don't say nothing. Teammates don't beat the crap out of each other 'cause they're a little jealous. Not even hockey players."

I swatted his hand away and growled. "He said something I didn't like."

Elliot went still. "Was it about me?"

I gave him a "What the fuck?" look. "You? No, why would he say anything about you?"

" 'Cause I'm queer."

I hesitated for a second and shook my head. "No. It wasn't about you."

"What was it, then?" When I didn't answer he tried again. "Was it about a girl?"

"No."

"A guy?"

"I don't—"

"Look, I know this has been weird for you, and I get that you have a strange way of showing allegiance but don't get in fights for me. I know how to defend myself and—"

I threw my hands in the air and stalked to the kitchen area. "Geez, it had nothing to do with you!"

"Okay. Sorry. That sounded paranoid. What was it about?"

My heart accelerated, my mouth went dry and the longer I stayed silent, the heavier the air got. When I thought it might choke me, I opened my mouth and blurted, "I'm bi."

Elliot closed the distance between us and sat on the barstool. "Huh? I don't get it."

"I'm bi too. There's nothing to get. It's just who I am, I guess."

"Why didn't you say something when I told you about me?"

" 'Cause I didn't know at first and then I didn't want it to be true. I thought I was curious because of what you were going through. And you seemed happy with Drew and geez, even the sex sounded good and—"

"You heard us having sex?" he asked, dropping his jaw like a cartoon character.

"Yeah. I did. I heard it and I'm sorry I didn't tell you, but I couldn't. And I'm sorry you thought I couldn't handle your gay stuff. That wasn't it. I was just going through my own stuff. It wasn't you, it was me. And it's still me."

"Hang on. Back up and tell me everything," he instructed.

I grabbed a package of frozen peas from the freezer and held it against my cheek as I filled Elliot in about my night from hell. "I feel so out of control, and I don't like it."

"No one likes that feeling," he said before adding, "So...you and Sky, eh? I feel like I should have guessed. He seems cool."

"He is. He's...fuck, I don't want to lose him."

"I get it, but you have choices, Colb. You can tell the truth or a half-truth or a lie. Sky isn't going to out you, Kendra doesn't really know the truth, and Schultz is a bully. You can tell your team whatever you want, and they'll believe you because you love the game. You're not in it for the glory. You play hockey because it's real and harsh and honest. And you put it before anything else in your life. Even yourself."

I set the peas down and kicked Elliot's chair. "I really am sorry. I'm a sucky friend, and I'm probably saying this way too late, but...I'm proud of you. You made it look so easy, and I know it wasn't easy at all."

"No, it wasn't easy. It was hard. But I couldn't live a lie anymore. That's what it felt like. Things didn't work out with Drew, but I'm not sorry I came out. It's a weight off my shoulders. And it feels good not to hide."

"I bet."

Elliot smacked my knee. "You should put some ice on your

lip too. You were never pretty, Colb, but you're downright ugly now."

"Fuck off," I huffed without heat. I flipped my cell over when it buzzed and read my incoming messages. I stood on shaky legs as a new round of panic gripped me.

Elliot snickered. "I'm kidding. C'mon, let's order pizza and turn on a hockey game and—"

"I can't. I have to go. Troy and Logan and a few of the guys want to come over. I can't be here."

"You're gonna leave me with them?"

"I told them I'll call them tomorrow, but I'm not taking any chances. Cover for me. I owe you one." I slugged his arm good-naturedly and headed for the door.

"Where are you going?"

"I don't know. I'll figure it out."

10

Driving aimlessly around Long Beach wasn't much of a plan. There was too much traffic, I was low on gas, and my phone wouldn't stop buzzing. Not to mention, my head hurt like a motherfucker. I found myself nearing the exit for my mom and Harry's house. Knowing my mom wasn't there made me second-guess showing up unannounced with a lame excuse about wanting to borrow a couple of Advil. I pulled to the curb, noting the porch light was on. Harry was up. He turned off the light before he went to bed. I used to mess with him sometimes and turn it off to bug him. It never worked. He'd always just laughed. Okay, so maybe this was a bad idea, I mused as my cell buzzed in my hand.

Don't ask me why I answered it. I was stalling, panicking, and nothing made sense, so why not chat with the loose cannon who set this mess in motion.

"Hi, Kendra," I answered.

"Colby! Oh, my God. I'm so sorry," she sobbed. "It's my fault. I did this. I hate him. He's so awful. I undid everything. No one knows, so don't freak out."

"What are you talking about?"

"I told everyone that Jason twisted my words. Troy was so mad, your coach was mad too, but they believed me. They know Sky and you are just friends. They said you're a hothead and that Jason stirs up shit. They said it made sense that you got so angry. They understand. It's fine now. I fixed it. Colby? Colby, are you there?"

"Yeah. I'm here." I swiped my hand across my nose and stared at the misty glow of the lamplight on the corner of the quiet street. "Thanks."

"There's a party tonight at Lawler's place in Bixby Village. You should come. A bunch of your teammates are going and… they're on your side." When I didn't say anything, she continued in a rush, "If you want, I'll make out with you in the kitchen where everyone can see us. We'll say Jason was jealous of you 'cause he knew I wanted you and…we can make up a story. They'll believe us, Colby. I know they will."

"Right. Um, thanks."

"Okay. I'll see you there."

"No, probably not," I replied. "Thanks, though. I'll see you at school."

I hung up before she could protest and glanced at the house again just as the porch light went off. I got out of the car and hurried toward the door. Harry opened it on the first knock.

"Well, hello! This is a nice surprise," Harry said, stepping aside to welcome me inside. "Your mom is away this weekend in Arizona. Are you hungry or thirsty? I have a—oh. What happened to your face?"

"Uh…"

"Let's get you some ice."

I dutifully followed him into the kitchen and let him fawn over me. Within ten minutes, I had an ice pack on my cheek and a cup of chamomile tea. I didn't want either, but I didn't feel like arguing, so I let him take over. He puttered around me, chattering about the weather in Arizona and a trip to the airport in the morning. I'd become an expert at tuning him out over the years.

I hummed in the right places and sipped tea while my brain churned on a medley of things that seemed so much bigger than me. I wondered what I'd do if my dad was still alive...if I could talk to him about Sky or my life. If it was just a matter of hockey, I knew the answer was yes. But life was so much more complicated now. I wasn't a kid anymore. And I had more on my mind than the game.

Which might have been why I didn't realize Harry had gone quiet. I glanced over the rim of my teacup and did a double take when I caught his concerned look.

"What's wrong?"

Harry smiled. "Not a thing. But if you have anything you'd like to talk about, I'm more than happy to lend an ear."

"No, I'm fine," I lied.

He nodded, then skirted the island and patted my shoulder. "All right. I need my beauty sleep. As you can tell, I've got a few years to catch up on. Lock the door when you leave and set the alarm and—"

"Can I stay?" someone who sounded like me blurted.

"Of course," he replied without hesitation. "I'll see you in the morning. I bought some wonderful croissants at the bakery. I'll make eggs and..."

He listed menu possibilities with a smile on his face like he actually didn't mind that I'd shown up out of the blue and asked to spend the night. He looked perfectly unfazed, like he had after every fucking tantrum I'd thrown as a teenager. How was that even possible?

"Harry, why do you do this?"

"Do what?"

"Why do you let me in and let me ruin your night? My mom

isn't even here. You don't have to be nice to me for her sake, so why don't you tell me to pull myself together? I wouldn't put up with me. Why do you?"

"Because I understand," he said simply.

"Geez, that's what Kendra said. She doesn't understand a thing, and I really doubt you do either. You've been married to Mom for a while but you don't know anything about me. Not really."

"I know the important things. I know you're a hard worker, a smart young man, a good friend, an excellent son, and you're a leader. What did I leave out?" he asked cheerfully.

I hopped from the barstool and paced to the bank of windows. Moonlight reflected off the pool and sparkled across the water like glitter. The sense of déjà vu hit me hard. I wished Sky was here. I wished we were naked in the hot tub, staring up at the stars, talking about superheroes and cartoons with our feet tangled. I wanted him. I wanted hockey. I wanted friends who would accept me for who I was. My dad used to tell me that setting goals was half the battle. But he hadn't been talking about real life. He'd been talking about hockey. And Harry...he still thought there were four quarters, and I'd heard him call a goalie a catcher more than once. So what did he understand exactly?

"You left out the part about being difficult, contrary, and an asshole in general."

"You're not an asshole, Colby. You're playing with the cards you've been dealt in the best way you know how. And when I say I understand, it's because I've been in your shoes too."

I furrowed my brow and huffed. "I don't think so. You're the happiest person I've ever met. If it's rainy, you say it's great for the garden. If your toast gets burned, you say you like the extra crunch. Nothing bugs you. Nothing. My life is screwed. Or maybe not. I don't know. I want something I can't have unless I give up the one thing I've always wanted. I don't know how to find the sunny side and get on with it. I'm nothing like you."

Harry cocked his head thoughtfully. "I didn't say we were alike. I said I understood. I've had my share of heartache. I've had dark days I wished would swallow me whole."

"When they canceled *Friends*?" I snarked.

"No. I lost my first wife and our five-year-old son in an accident thirty years ago."

"Oh. Geez, Harry, I'm sorry. I didn't know. You never said anything and—"

"Why would I tell a young man who's grieving about my own loss? You lost your hero, Colby. You lost your home and your sense of stability. I know what that feels like. I understand your pain. I've felt your pain. But it's not my place to tell you how to grieve or how to cope. I can only assure you that you aren't alone and that you have my support no matter what. I'm not your father. I don't want to take his place. But if I can help you, I will. I'll open my home, my wallet, my refrigerator...whatever you need. No questions asked. If you have anything you want to share, I'm more than happy to listen."

"Why?"

"Because once upon a time, good people listened to me. Some offered friendship or a shoulder to cry on, a few offered their sofa when I couldn't bear to go home to a quiet house. I'm grateful. And I'm not just willing to help you, I *want* to help you. If I can—"

"I'm bi," I blurted.

"Okay."

"And I'm with someone. A guy. He's important to me," I continued cautiously.

"Sky?"

"How did you know?"

Harry pointed at his eyes and winked. "I see things. You're not as sneaky as you think."

If he told me there were cameras in Bailey's office, I might actually vomit. I gave him a shaky smile instead.

"Oh?"

"You're both rather smitten. It's easy to see if you're looking. It's easy to ignore if you're not. Your mom was wondering when—"

"My mom knows?" I raked my hand through my hair and started pacing again.

"She doesn't know for sure. But she's rather sensitive to your happiness. She's noticed you've been…"

"Less of a dick?" I supplied.

Harry chuckled lightly. "Something like that. Does your black eye have anything to do with your news?"

"Sort of." I touched the tender skin under my left eye, then sank into a barstool and told him everything.

"Sounds like nothing has to change if you go to that party tonight. Is that right?" he asked gently.

"Maybe, but…I don't want to go."

"You can straighten it out with your team tomorrow or Monday. You have a friend to cover for you and Sky won't stand in your way, so—"

"But that isn't what I want."

"Hmm. What's stopping you from going after everything you want? Obviously, it's fear. But what are you afraid of? Your team's reaction, losing your friends, losing family? You're not a fear-driven person. You like to rock the boat. What's stopping you?"

I pursed my lips hard, but I couldn't keep the tears at bay. My eyes welled and my throat closed. I swallowed around the ball of emotion and looked away.

"My dad. He wouldn't like this. He didn't want me to be like this. He wanted me to be better than him. A better skater, a better athlete…it was all about hockey and hockey players aren't gay," I choked.

Harry didn't speak immediately. He let my words linger in the air between us until they dissipated and evaporated. Then he leaned forward and gave me a sharp look.

"You know that isn't true, Colby. And you know your dad loved you more than he loved the game. The game was his connection to you. It was currency. Something to talk about when distance threatened to pull you apart. It wasn't a measure of love. You know that."

"Every message is about hockey. I listened to them so often. 'Hey buddy, practice hard. Hey buddy, get a hat trick for me. Hey buddy, I want you to kick ass at your game today.' None of them are about me. So, I've been waiting for a sign from him to let me know he wouldn't give up on me or think I was weak if I admit…"

"If you admit what?" he prodded.

"That I'm in love with a guy," I whispered.

"Hmm. What does your gut tell you?"

I licked my lips and let out a ragged breath. "I want Sky."

Harry lifted his brow then smiled and gathered my teacup before heading for the sink to rinse it out. He squeezed my arm as he passed and said goodnight. I think he mentioned something about the alarm and maybe bacon too, but my head was spinning again. But in a good way.

If anyone told me I'd spend an entire Sunday hanging out with Harry and my mother of my own free will, I'd have said they were high. But I did. I picked up my mom from the airport with Harry after breakfast and went shopping for succulents. Mom put me to work planting in the garden while she bored me to tears with stories about my aunt's family and cousins I hadn't seen in years. But at one point she crouched beside me wearing her big floppy gardening hat and a pair of gloves and bumped my elbow.

"Just so we're clear, I like him. A lot."

"Who? Harry?"

"I love Harry," she gushed, chuckling when I rolled my eyes. "But I like Sky. And I love you. Be happy, my darling."

I smiled, then tickled her until she quit giving me gooey looks. And later that night, after I'd texted my friends and my coach and assured them I was relatively sane and that I'd be at practice Monday, I started making a new plan.

TODAY WAS AN ICE DAY. I had more reservations about making a scene on the ice than I did about saying the words. This was holy ground to me. This was where I came to do battle. To fight and to win. Not to talk about my fucking feelings. But this wasn't about feelings. It was about truth. And it wasn't until I'd strapped my skates on that it struck me as poetic and kind of perfect to tell my truth here. I did a couple of laps to warm up. I didn't put my earpods in. I needed to be completely aware of my surroundings...the cut of the blades on the pristine ice, the echo of the AC unit, and the hum of distant conversation. The noise was getting louder. It was almost time.

"Hey, why aren't you in the locker room? Get your gear on," Troy said, adjusting his face mask. "And let's make this apology process painless, please. You look a hell of a lot better than Schultz. Did you see his stitches?"

"No, I didn't. I just—"

"Yo, Fischer!" Coach motioned me over.

I spotted Schultz at his side and cautioned myself to relax. I knew what I was doing. I was okay. He wasn't my story.

I gave what I thought might pass for a smile as I came to a stop against the board.

"Hi, Coach."

"You got something to say?" he asked in a stern paternal growl.

"Yeah. I apologize for the other night."

"Good. Apologize to the team and we'll put this behind us. They'll be out in a minute. By the way, you're both suspended for two games. But I expect you to practice your asses off. Get your gear on, Fischer, and—"

"Yeah, but I have something else to say."

"You don't have to say anything. We're not rehashing that shit show. You two handle it between yourselves like adults," Coach said as the team hopped onto the ice like ducklings one after the other. He blew his whistle to gather everyone around him and gave a terse speech about respect, responsibility, and sportsmanship before pointing at Schultz and me. "These two are going to say they're sorry, then we're getting to work. Make it short and sweet. I'm going to pull out some more cones. Finish up here and start a half-ice passing drill, Fischer."

Schultz glared at me when Coach turned away. I studied the row of stitches above his eyebrow as he choked out a jumbled apology. That had to hurt.

"Sorry about the face, Fish."

"I'm not." I held up my hand and took a deep breath. This was it. "I'm glad Schultz said what he did. I'm glad I got mad. The timing wasn't great. It shouldn't have happened during a game. I apologize for the lapse in judgment. It was selfish and irresponsible. But he was right. I'm bi."

"What the fuck?" Troy gaped.

"You heard me. It doesn't change who I am or how hard I

play. It's just something you might want to know or maybe you don't. But I don't want to deal with rumors and backstabbing. When I'm on the ice, I'm here to play hockey. I'm here to work. My personal life has nothing to do with my skills. I don't plan on quitting. I don't plan on fading into the background. I just thought you might want to hear the truth from me."

Silence.

No one said a word. I listened for the echoes and hums, but I couldn't hear a thing above the sound of my heartbeat. I scanned my teammates' shocked faces...Troy, Logan, Ramirez... even Schultz looked surprised. I wondered what else I could possibly say, but I didn't owe them any more than I'd already given. I scratched my head just as Troy spoke up.

"Captain, what drill are we starting with?"

I smiled my thanks and barked out a set of orders before gliding onto the ice.

THE OFFICE SEEMED BUSIER than usual for a late Monday afternoon. I'd hoped for a minor miracle...like everyone calling in sick at the same time. Minus the germy element, of course. I'd never done anything like this, and the thought of having an audience made me even more nervous than I already was. But this was a "go big or go home" moment.

I flung my cape behind me as I stepped up to the reception desk. "Hey, Meg. Is Sky in?"

"Yeah, he—oh. Holy cannoli, Batman! What's happening here? Are we still celebrating Halloween? Not that I'm complaining. You look...incredible."

"Thanks. Sky?" I asked, inclining my head toward the main office area.

"Do you want me to announce you or—"

"No. Just tell where he's sitting now."

"He's at your old desk. Go get 'em, big guy," she said, beaming a bright smile at me.

I moved quickly around the maze of cubicles, pausing to give a high five or two as I made my way around the perimeter. I got a few catcalls and a round of applause. I'd obviously misjudged the excitement level a geeky costume would raise in a roomful of accountants. Sue craned her neck from her desk, Scott from IT popped out of the copy room, and when I turned the corner to my old cubby, Sky was there.

He leaned on the wall with a curious expression, looking sexier than anyone should in standard-issue khakis and a plain blue oxford shirt. He uncrossed his arms and furrowed his brow as I closed the distance.

"Batman?"

"Yes. That's me. Can I talk to you in private...please?" I pleaded, gesturing at the looky-loos chuckling at my getup behind me.

"Um. Where do you want to go? Harry's using the conference room, Bailey and Barnes are both here, and Jake must have eaten something funky at lunch, 'cause he's been in the bathroom all afternoon and—"

I held up my hand like a stop sign. "TMI. This will have to do."

"Okay. What's this about?" he asked, gesturing at my costume.

"Me and you and..."

"What does Batman have to do with us?"

"Nothing. But you like Batman."

"I do," he replied cautiously.

"He's your favorite. You told me he was your favorite months ago."

"Okay. Well, that's true, but what does that—"

"I want to be your favorite," I said quickly. "Me. Get it?"

"What are you saying?"

"I came out."

Sky gaped at me. "You did?"

"Yeah. Just happened, so it's a little surreal. But I told Harry and my mom and Elliot. And my team. I don't want to hide anymore. I can't keep all these balls in the air. I don't want to lie to protect myself. I'd rather fight and be honest. I didn't mention you to my guys. You don't have to come out if you don't want to, but...I want you to know that I love you."

Sky threw his arms around my neck and crashed his mouth over mine. He pushed my mask over my head and threaded his fingers through my hair.

"I love you too." Sky brushed his nose against mine and chuckled. "Why Batman?"

"Because there's a serious lack of Green Lantern costumes in the world," I huffed. I let the sound of Sky's laughter roll over me in sweet waves before I continued. "Batman seemed logical...sort of. I guess I wanted you to know that I've been listening to you for months now. And I see you. I know your lip curls on the right side when you get angry. And when you're happy, your eyes crinkle and you become a grown-up version of the kid who wants to catch up on everything he's missed. I want to make sure you don't miss anything else. You're first for me. Everything else is second. Got it?"

"Got it." He bit my lip and grinned. "I love you, but I'm not Robin."

"Fine. *You* can be Green Lantern."

Sky snickered. "No, thanks."

I draped my arm over his shoulder and kissed his temple, then grumbled about my sweaty balls and the danger of my junk being confined in polyester for too long. Sky wrapped his arms around my waist and laughed.

And just like that, I had my sign. The one I'd been waiting for since I was fifteen. I closed my eyes for a brief moment, tilted my chin toward the heavens, and smiled.

Maybe the heavens approved, maybe they didn't. I wasn't overly concerned either way. Somehow I knew I was on the right path with the right man. I wasn't afraid. I was free. I'd learned the hard way to trust my instincts and come out on the ice.

EPILOGUE

"I have so much of you in my heart."—John Keats

COUPLES SHOULDN'T grocery shop together. Only one person from each household needed to go to the market at any given time. It should be a rule, right? I steered my cart through the paper goods section at Costco and stopped in front of the jumbo container of plastic utensils. I sincerely doubted we'd need three hundred forks for our barbeque, but I dropped them on top of the huge box of oatmeal anyway.

"Those are bad for the environment, babe. We'll get the real thing," Sky said, scratched my lower back, then moved down the aisle, pausing to pick up a package of napkins.

"Wait a sec. How many people are coming over?"

"Twenty-five...ish," he replied with a smile.

"Are you proposing that we buy twenty-five real forks for a bunch of knucklehead baseball dudes and a few hockey players?"

"I am." Sky chuckled. "Why do you look so scandalized? They aren't too pricey, and we're both making good money. We can afford to own more than four forks."

"But why would we? And what the hell are we gonna do with an extra twenty we'll never use? Should we just tell our friends to take a fork home like a fuckin' party favor or something?"

Sky threw his head back and laughed. "This is a family zone, Fischer. Watch your language. And no. We're not giving forks away. We'll have them for a rainy day. This is our first official get-together. There will be others. Oh, we need cheese for the burgers and I'm not sure I have all the ingredients for tofu patties and—"

"Tofu what? Stop everything." I held my hand up like a traffic cop and shook my head. "This has to be an alternate reality moment. You did not just suggest we serve tofu to a bunch of athletes. They'll hurt us."

"You're afraid to serve tofu?"

"Hell yes, I am! And don't try to tell me it tastes like the real thing. It does not."

"When was the last time you had tofu?" he asked, clearly amused.

"I was sixteen and I'm still scarred," I snarked, slinging my arm over his shoulder and nuzzling his neck. "This is why you should have let me do the shopping. I could have been outta here ten minutes ago with everything we needed."

"Yeah right," he huffed. "You would have come home with three hundred plastic forks, ground beef, and some buns. There's more to a barbeque than plain ol' hamburgers. We need condiments, fruit, and maybe we should do vegetable skewers, and corn, and..."

I let his melodic voice wash over me. He was literally reciting a grocery list, and it was the biggest freaking turn-on. And no, it had nothing to do with food. It was more a sense of belonging.

He was mine, and that was our grocery list. *Our* friends were coming to *our* housewarming party. And yeah, if Sky wanted to serve tofu, it was okay by me.

I wanted to pinch myself sometimes because my life didn't seem real. So much had changed over the past few months. For once, it was all good.

Sky came out to his teammates immediately after I did. Baseball wasn't in season at the time, so for him, it was a matter of making a few phone calls or meeting with a couple of guys to apologize for how he handled their coming out, like his ex, Max, and his former roommate, Christian. I sat beside him and held his hand under the table at Starbucks, quietly admiring his strength and poise. He'd fallen short or fallen down time and again, but he kept showing up and he kept fighting. He might have lost his family, but he'd gained a new one. His coworkers at BBC, my mom and Harry, his teammates, hell…even my friends and teammates rallied around him.

We had more love and support in our lives than we'd thought possible. It wasn't all smooth sailing by any stretch. Not everyone was cool and accepting, but those people didn't define us. And in some ways, they made us stronger. We'd learned to appreciate honesty and to stand up for our own truths.

Part of my truth was that I'd most likely never play professional hockey. That would have been a bitter pill to swallow a year ago, but there were other ways to be "the best" on the ice. I started coaching the Pee Wee hockey team at the rink after my season ended and liked it more than I thought I would. I split my time between the ice and school and Sky's baseball games.

His season was over at the end of April, unless they made the playoffs. We figured we'd squeeze our barbeque in before we had to compete with games and graduations. We'd moved in together in January, so we were already a few months late. Not that our friends minded. It was a busy time of year, but it looked like we'd have a good turnout. Friends from both of our teams would be there, Elliot and his new guy, and yeah, even Kendra. But I was reasonably sure none of them wanted a tofu burger.

I hooked my fingers through Sky's belt loop and tugged so he bumped against my chest. "What if we double up on veggies and forget the tofu?"

He leaned into my side and smiled. "Deal. But I still want real forks."

I let out a faux put-upon sigh. "It's a good thing I love you."

He hugged me impulsively and pinched my side. "I love you too, Colb."

And yes, Sky was the other part of my truth. My main truth. He was the only sign I needed. My reason, my heart, my soul. I believed in us. And I believed in our future.

OUT IN COLLEGE SERIES

Out in College is my new adult series set in Southern California. Each book has a sports theme and though some characters will be feature in other stories, these books can be read on their own and in any order. So far, we've got water polo, football, baseball, ice hockey. And coming soon...volleyball!

Check out the entire series, beginning with water polo with Derek and Gabe's story in ***Out in the Deep****, Book 1...*

Football with Evan and Mitch in ***Out in the End Zone****, Book 2...*

A little more football with Christian and Rory in ***Out in the Offense****, Book 3...*

Some baseball with Max and Phoenix in ***Out in Field****, Book 4...*

Ice hockey in ***Out on the Ice****, Book 5. And yes, Book 6 will be here in Summer 2020!*

STARTING FROM SERIES

Don't miss my new rock and roll series! Book 1 begins with a song and Book 2 is about the record deal.

Starting From Zero, *Book 1*

Justin Cuevas is going through a rough patch. A broken relationship, a scandal, and the demise of his band have shaken the aspiring rock star's confidence. With a little luck, he's hoping to re-launch his music career in LA with his new band, Zero. The key is to stay focused, and not get distracted by his past...or the sexy songwriter he can't get out of his head.

Gray Robertson has written dozens of hits and worked with some of the biggest names in the industry. But he's never met anyone like Justin. The younger man is fiery, passionate, and smart. A powerful voice for a new generation. Other than an unforgettable one-night stand and a passion for music, the two men have nothing in common. Or do they?

***Starting From Scratch**, Book 2*

Charlie Rourke is an ultra fabulous human whirlwind on a mission to launch the next biggest band in the world. However, he might have taken on more than he could handle when he signed on to manage Zero.

Ky Baldwin loves a challenge as much as anyone, but Charlie doesn't make things easy. Zero's manager is a force of nature and Ky can't stop thinking about him.

COMING SOON! STARTING FROM HERE - SPRING 2020

EXCERPT FROM STARTING FROM HERE - SPRING 2020

I regarded Declan for a moment then shrugged my shirt off my shoulders and draped it over the sofa. “Well, you know where the door is.”

“Yeah, but I’m not going anywhere until we get a couple of things straight. We need to move on so we don’t fuck this up for everyone around us. It’s two songs, T. It won’t take much time. We can do this Monday and you can go back to ignoring me on Tuesday.”

“Unless they suck,” I snarked.

“They don’t. They’re rockin’ tunes with sweet melodies.” He paused hum a few bars then glanced around the room. He eyed the bass on a stand against the wall before refocusing on me. “I can send you a sample, but it’s probably easier for you to walk into our side of the studio and hear us live. You know it’s all about the nuances. You have a good sense of when to add something extra to the beat and when to hold back. What d’ya say?”

“I’ll think about it.” I gave him a phony smile then took another swig of my beer, and set the bottle on the table before casually moving past him to open the door.

“I need to know by Monday.”

"Hmm. I'll keep that in mind," I replied noncommittedly.

He narrowed his eyes. "This isn't a joke, you know."

"I didn't say it was."

"That's 'cause you're not saying anything at all."

"Gee, and I thought I'd been exceedingly clear that I didn't want to fuckin' talk to you."

Dec gripped the edge of the door and slammed it shut with enough force to rattle the windows before rounding on me angrily.

"I hate that you can't admit it was your fault too."

"*My* fault?" I huffed incredulously.

"Yes!" He growled, gesturing toward my bedroom wildly. "It happened here, Tegan. This is where it started. This is a fucking crime scene! There were witnesses. Don't tell me I imagined you and Justin and—"

"Enough!" I backed him against the wall and put my hand over his mouth. I let go to brace my arms on either side of his head, caging him in, so he no choice but to listen. "Your memory sucks. This isn't where it started. This was where it ended. You know it and I know it. Don't try to rewrite history. We both know the real story."

Declan didn't move, but his gaze darted from my mouth to my eyes like he was looking for something. Or remembering something. He licked his bottom lip and let out a pained sound…part anger, part frustration.

"Do we?"

I nodded slightly then tentatively set my thumb over his bottom lip. If he asked what the fuck I was doing, I'd tell him I wanted to shut him up. But the truth was…I was overcome with a rush of emotion I couldn't name. It wasn't anger, but it had the same bite. Like getting vicious pangs in a bakery when you're on a diet. The smell alone was sweet torture. A reminder of something that tasted so good, but was so bad for you.

Temptation is a wicked thing though. It draws you in and pulls you under. One moment you're standing on the outside looking in behind a carefully constructed barrier, and the next...

I inched forward, so close that my nose skimmed the end of his. I breathed him in, drawing his intoxicating scent deep inside my lungs. He smelled so...manly. Woodsy, but fresh. And hauntingly familiar.

But I didn't like ghosts. They knew shit about you and they never let go.

"We do. And that story is over now," I said in a gravelly voice.

Declan cocked his head and smiled. One of those slow-moving roguish grins that made me feel funny inside. He'd always had a way of asserting control, even when he was the one with his back to the wall. So, maybe I should have seen it coming. Maybe I should have clued into the red flashing warning signs and the alarm bells ringing in my ear. But I couldn't see clearly and I couldn't hear a thing over the insistent drumming of my heart against my chest.

"I don't think so, T. I think it's just begun."

ABOUT THE AUTHOR

Lane Hayes is grateful to finally be doing what she loves best. Writing full-time! It's no secret Lane loves a good romance novel. An avid reader from an early age, she has always been drawn to well-told love story with beautifully written characters. These days she prefers the leading roles to both be men. Lane discovered the M/M genre a few years ago and was instantly hooked. Her debut novel was a 2013 Rainbow Award finalist and subsequent books have received Honorable Mentions, and were winners in the 2016, 2017, and 2018-2019 Rainbow Awards. She loves red wine, chocolate and travel (in no particular order). Lane lives in Southern California with her amazing husband in a newly empty nest.

***Join Lane's reading group, Lane's Lovers for immediate updates!**

ALSO BY LANE HAYES

Out in the Deep

Out in the End Zone

Out in the Offense

Out in the Field

Starting From Zero

Starting From Scratch

Stick to the Script (Ace's Wild Series #13)

Leaning Into Love

Leaning Into Always

Leaning Into the Fall

Leaning Into a Wish

Leaning Into Touch

Leaning Into the Look

Leaning Into Forever

Better Than Good

Better Than Chance

Better Than Friends

Better Than Safe

Better Than Beginnings (A Matt & Aaron Short Story Collection)

A Kind of Truth

A Kind of Romance

A Kind of Honesty

A Kind of Home

The Right Words

The Wrong Man

The Right Time

A Way with Words

A Way with You

Made in the USA
Columbia, SC
18 June 2025